What Are the Chances?

Also by Robert Scotellaro

Anthology

NEW MICRO:
Exceptionally Short Fiction
Co-edited with James Thomas

Fiction

Nothing Is Ever One Thing
Bad Motel
What We Know So Far
Measuring the Distance

Poetry

After the Revolution
The Night Sings A Capella
Rhapsody of Fallen Objects
My Father's Cadillac
Early Love Poems of Genghis Khan
Blinded by Halos
East Harlem Poems

For Children

Snail Stampede
Dancing with Frankenstein
Carla and the Greedy Merchant
The Terrible Storm

WHAT ARE *the* CHANCES?

flash fictions

Robert Scotellaro

Press 53
Winston-Salem

Press 53, LLC
PO Box 30314
Winston-Salem, NC 27130

First Edition

Cover design by Claire V. Foxx

Cover art, "Knolling Colorful Collection Vintage Dice,"
Copyright © 2017 by cglade, licensed through iStock

Author photo by Diana Scott

Library of Congress Control Number
2020940126

Printed on acid-free paper
ISBN 978-1-950413-26-3

for Diana

Grateful acknowledgment is made to the following publications in which these stories or earlier versions previously appeared:

Airgonaut: A Journal of Short Fiction: "Break Dancing Butcher," "Those Eyes in the Rearview"

Bad Motel: "What Remains"

Bending Genres Journal: "Ouch! (A Love Story)"

Best Microfiction 2020 (Guest Edited by Michael Martone): "Hit Man in Retirement"

Best Small Fictions, 2016 (Guest Edited by Stuart Dybek): "Bug Porn"

Best Small Fictions, 2017 (Guest Edited by Amy Hempel): "What Remains"

Blink Ink: "Somewhere Beneath It"

Blue Fifth Review: "A Rush of Shadows," "Rock-A-Bye," "Oven Gloves," "Dear God (A Love Story)"

Burnside Review: "Martians, Chili Lime Pistachios, and What Was Left of My Father"

Connotation Press: "Schadenfreude Makes Me Horny"

District Lit Magazine: "A Unicorn, a Chicken, and God Speaking Through My Mother's Cat"

Fast Forward (Volume 2): "Book of Facts"

Fast Forward (Volume 3): "Mr. Nasty"

Fast Forward (Volume 4): "Fun House"

Flash Boulevard: "Lion's Head Meatballs," "How to Build a God," "Little Castles," "The Room Next Door," "Worth Tasting," "Soliloquy"

Flash Fiction International (W.W. Norton anthology): "Fun House"

Flash Frontier: "Fly Swatter" (*Best Small Fictions, 2018* finalist, Guest Edited by Aimee Bender)

Flash: The International Short-Short Story Magazine: "Not Even Ed Sullivan Could Save Sundays," "Leaping," "Crazy Hats," "Broken Tale," "Wise Sunglasses," "The Horns," "Safe"

Freshwater Literary Journal: "Something for Henrietta," "No Peeking," "Water in Still Life"

Funny Bone Anthology: "A Penchant for Renegades"

Gargoyle: "Bad-Boy Wannabe and the Cephalopod Empire"

Great Jones Street: "A Disadvantage of Momentum," "Fun House," "What Are the Chances?" (originally, "A Knife On the Bed")

Journal of Compressed Creative Arts (Matter Press): "His Ink and Miss Atomic Bomb (In Triptych)," "What Are the Chances?" (originally, "A Knife On the Bed")

Measuring the Distance: "Mr. Nasty," "Fun House," "The Cleaning Girl," "Book of Facts," "Flatware" (originally, "A Fork in the Neck")

Mojave River Review: "The Polygamist's Three Wives"

NANOFiction/NANO Fiction Podcast: "Leaning In"

National Flash-Fiction Day 2018 Anthology: "The Polygamist's Three Wives"

National Flash-Fiction Day 2019 Anthology: "The Pencil"

New Flash Fiction Review: "Paper Dolls," "A Lamb at the Dinner Table," "Fun House"

Pure Slush: "Fake Eunuch"

Spelk Fiction: "The Tiniest Fish," "Hit Man in Retirement"

What We Know So Far: "The Polygamist's Three Wives," "Bug Porn," "Superhero, "The Interview," "A Purgatory Dweller's Guide to Bird-Watching"

Contents

I prefer winter and fall, when you feel the bone structure of the landscape. Something waits beneath it, the whole story doesn't show.

—Andrew Wyeth

THE TINIEST FISH

B en mentioned his job at the rubber ball factory, and she told him how that would explain why he bounced back so quickly. He liked that, and let her know it with his best Bozo the Clown smile, all dusted off after leaving his wife of twenty-four years for another woman, and the woman leaving *him* for another man.

It reminded him of a cartoon he'd seen as a kid, of a small fish being swallowed whole by a bigger fish, then a bigger fish swallowing that one, and so on. . . Till the last fish was enormous. There was always a bigger fish waiting.

They were in a hot tub at a roadside motel, under a corrugated plastic overhang, and it was raining. "But what I really do," he said, "I mean, where my heart is, is writing novels."

"Really," she said. "You write a bestseller?"

"Well, it's just one. Not published yet. But I have an agent." He pulled his hand from the bubbling tub. "Fingers crossed," he said.

"What's it about?"

"It's called *The Zombie in Fishnet Stockings*. Kind of a zombie romance/detective thriller."

She nodded, turned away, a bit distracted. She was wearing a skimpy bikini and he noticed the faint imprint of a small cross at the crest of a sunburnt breast.

"Zombies," she said. "Huh."

"They're popular," he said. "Who knows, maybe it'll be a series. TV—eventually."

"I'll look for it," she said, then added, "when the time comes." There was a sudden downpour and they both looked up. "You ever think how this is the same rain that fell on Cleopatra," he said. "I mean, obviously we're not in Egypt and it's not thousands of years ago. But it's the same rain that's been around forever. Just circulating, continuously. I've always found that fascinating."

She looked around again. "Huh?"

"It just keeps going up and coming down. The same old stuff. Pretty cool actually." He couldn't believe he used the word "cool." Thought he sounded like one of his kids. Especially the youngest.

"That never occurred to me," she said, and as she glanced up, a man with an umbrella put two towels off to the side and slipped into the water beside her. "Umm," he said and gave her a long kiss, then leaned back, stretching his legs out. And there was that crucifix on a chain, nestled in a clump of chest hair.

Ben moved over and let one of the jets blow out against his back. It was pretty sore from all those road miles he was racking up. The *adventure*s he promised himself.

In the cartoon, a man in a boat caught the enormous fish. But when he reeled it in beaming (his pole tautly bent) each fish slipped away one by one back into the water, till the man stared in dismay at the tiny fish that was left.

Ben eased out of the tub and headed back to his room. He could feel the cold needle pricks against his skin. There'd be some beer and a pack of cigarettes waiting. And as for the rain: hell, if it was good enough for Cleopatra or Genghis Khan on a wet horse, who the hell was he to complain?

PAPER DOLLS

The slick booklets are spread out, and he is looking at snapshots of young women. (My father, late in life: four wives later, two in the ground—my mother was his first.) Hundreds of them, coquettish in uniform squares. From the Philippines, China, Russia. Mail-order brides at the starting gate ready to beat a path to his door. To cook his food, fill his bed, sit with him in front of the TV, asking him, "What's this?" and, "What's that?" Mentor, guide, sage authority— their feet, their brightly painted toenails, up on his coffee table.

"Get real," I tell him as he turns the page, stabbing a finger against a smiling face. "A beaut," he says. "One better than the next. And don't be such a damn crepe hanger."

I duck through the flypaper coils dangling from light fixtures, high molding, floor lamps—everywhere in his small apartment. A hanging garden of dead things. Leave a bag of groceries on the table. He is sweating on the couch with every window open. There's a dumpster out back two stories below. Each window, a smiling invitation.

"Why don't you just get some screens?"

"Yeah, yeah." He picks up a handful of Chinese women this time. Glossy with hope and dreams big as his own. I'd given up pushing him to get an air conditioner. Even offered to pay for one. But he'd rather sweat and navigate the lushness of his hanging glue traps than watch a penny's worth of electricity fly out of the wall.

He writes them. At the kitchen table. Drinking beer and belching into the ink. Flowery ink for each. Blues and reds and purples... They write back in broken English on scented paper, and he keeps them in a row (in envelopes with odd stamps) between the toaster and his coffee maker. The exotic beauties he'll never meet. That chorus line there for him each morning as he looks up from his scrambled eggs. Pen and fork, interchangeable. Listening to the buzzing, then the silence. The buzzing, then the silence.

THOSE EYES
IN THE REARVIEW

The Uber driver didn't respond when I buckled up and said, "Hi." As he pulled away I saw his eyes in the rearview. They were red and crazed. An anonymous GPS voice said: "Go to Albion Street, then turn left. . ." He switched it off.

"You okay?" I said.

"I killed the fucker," he said. He was driving fast and was beginning to sob intermittently. "I'm pretty fucking far from okay!"

"What are you talking about? Hey, slow down." He didn't.

"I caught them *doing it*. In the middle of it. In our bed! I put a knife in his neck and then—I don't know—everywhere."

"Pull over," I said. "We'll talk." I was planning on leaping out the minute he stopped.

"Screw that," he said, and the eyes in the rearview were wet and angry.

"Is she. . .?"

"No, but she was screaming her head off when I ran out of there."

My mind was like one of those friction cars spinning out against a wall. Not going anywhere, just making a lot of noise in there. "Why the hell did you pick me up?"

He turned then, as he went through a crosswalk, and a woman with a bag of groceries stopped suddenly. He had a gun pointed at me. "You're my hostage," he said, then turned back. He put the gun beside him on the seat and both hands back on the wheel.

It's hard to know how you'll react in a crisis. In a life and death situation. My heart was going so fast I could hear it. I wanted to be calm, at least act calm—to talk calmly, see if I could reach him in some way, but what happened was, I screamed "Fuck!" released my seatbelt and tried to open the door. Not sure if I'd jump out at that speed or not, but all reason had left me, and all I knew was the outside seemed better than inside.

"It's locked," he said.

That's when I sat back, realized I was in the jaws of some crazy animal trap, and if I couldn't chew my leg off to escape, I had to reach him somehow.

"I've got kids," I said. "I've got nothing to do with all this."

"I know," he said. "But you're in it now."

I knew they'd catch up with him as we entered the freeway. I knew how this worked. They'd have a police helicopter and Highway Patrol checking makes of cars and license plates. He'd be cornered at some point, surrounded. There'd be a shootout. Probably what he wanted anyway on some level. Suicide by cop, only bullets go every which way. Weren't fussy about where they wound up.

"If I'm a hostage, then you'll want to call someone, let them know you want to negotiate. It was a crime of passion," I heard myself say. "They can cut you some slack with a thing like that. People do all kinds of things in a situation like that. That counts. You can make a deal."

He began to laugh. It wasn't the laugh of a madman on the brink. "That's a good one," he said, slowing down and getting in the exit lane. "*Let's Make a Deal*. My mom used to watch that show on TV." His demeanor was completely changed. His eyes in the rearview were bright and dry. "That was good, right?" he said. "Come on, you know I aced it."

And in an instant he went from desperate killer to wiseass. And I went from soon-to-be-deceased innocent victim to near-murderous passenger. "You fucking *what?*"

"Aced it," he said. Held up the gun. "Fake," he said. "You think this is what I'm gonna be doing for the rest of my life? I got star quality."

My heart was still going pretty good. My jaw swung open, but nothing came out.

"I'm heading for L.A. next week. I got an agent and everything." Exiting the highway, he turned the wheel with one hand down a street I recognized. We were only minutes from my destination.

"Are you fucking kidding me? This was all some kind of joke?"

"Hell no," he said. "That was some serious business, my friend. My *real* business. That was some top-notch acting, right? Come on, give me that."

"What I ought to give you is a punch in the mouth."

"I wouldn't try that," he said, and those eyes in the rearview were dangerous again. "I'm a black belt. Before you could get a hand up, I'd push your nose through your brain."

At a stop sign he glared at me for a long moment. Then that rubbery face changed yet again. "Only shittin'," he said. "I'm a wimp. But I *will* sue the shit out of you in a heartbeat. Come on," he said. "Lighten up. Consider it a sacrifice for the arts. I'll thank you at the Oscars one day." He nodded like a bobble doll, and I believed he believed that.

"Here ya go," he said, as he glided over in front of my dentist's office.

I looked at him, stunned, nearly numb. He pressed a button and I was able to open the door and get out. He waved. In my stupor I nearly waved back. Then I realized I had completely forgotten about my tooth hurting as it started up again, and I climbed the stairs, oddly grateful for the small matter it was.

NO PEEKING

He wore his tie as a blindfold when he visited his sightless friend. Tightened it over his eyes right before knocking. The blind friend told him to have a seat, he'd get them some brews, and he felt ashamed when he stumbled around a bit, bumping into things. Had to peek to see where the couch was.

When the blind friend handed him the cold bottle, he was surprised at how different it felt. The sudden focus on the chilled glass. The cold, slick label he picked at with his fingernail.

There was a fight on TV, and he heard *Perez* mentioned. Something about a strong left hook.

"Hey, thanks for coming," the blind friend said. "This guy's got some left. Doesn't seem like the layoff's hurt him any."

There was a pause as they both lifted their beers. He could hear himself chugging—the excited commentator's voice rising louder and louder.

"How's Marie?" his friend asked.

Christ, he thought. This never tasted better. He had half the label peeled. "Oh, she's fine. Out buying a new pair of shoes. Like the five hundred pairs she's already got aren't enough." They both laughed.

He could hear Edgar in his cage fluttering about on its newspaper flooring. "Looks like Edgar's a fight fan too," he said.

"He's just excited to see you is all."

It was between rounds and they listened in on a trainer ranting furiously, telling his guy to get his shit together. To clinch when he got tagged like that. "You can take this guy," he said.

The blindfolded man was getting tangled up in this new dark universe: the announcer, the crowd, Edgar's loud chatter, his blind friend guzzling. . .

"How you like my new shirt?" the blind man asked. Friend of mine brought it back from Hawaii."

"Nice," he heard himself say quickly. "It's got pizzazz." He thought to peek again, but felt he wanted to stick with this thing. Get a sense of what it might be like. The announcer was calling the fight again, and the crowd was getting loud.

"He packs a punch," the blind friend said. "That Perez is a real banger."

"I can see that," he said, wishing he could see that. It was like Edgar was watching the fight too. Getting louder, it seemed, along with the crowd.

"It's just a matter of time," his blind friend said. "Well, cheers."

"Cheers," he said back, then suddenly wondered if his friend was holding out his bottle for a clink. *Shit!* He lifted the tie up over one eye, and there was his friend in his boxer shorts, and nothing else, sitting across from him, smiling. Perez was on the mat, and Edgar was pecking away joyfully at a seed bar. He slipped the tie down, and tucked it under his collar. Leaned back and drained his beer.

The next fight—the main event—was pretty bland by comparison. A couple of chunky heavyweights. Mostly waltzing around the ring. Even Edgar didn't seem all that interested.

THE POLYGAMIST'S
THREE WIVES

The commune stood between a vast stretch of scrub oaks.
A land purring with haiku few noticed. The three women
sat in the kitchen around a pie one of them had baked.
Realized each of them had been faking orgasms. The youngest
one blushed. The middle wife was suddenly taken with the
blades of the ceiling fan. The eldest spit out a bit of pie as
she laughed, which the baby on her lap stabbed with a finger
and ate.

He sat in the next room. Looked over imperiously and
smiled. He was playing chess with his oldest, and not knowing
which piece to move, he moved his coffee cup from one
coffee ring to another. Off the kitchen was the clomping
sound of sneakers jogging around in the dryer, mixed with
the wives' laughter. A bee flew in one window and out another,
preferring the roses.

A LAMB AT THE
DINNER TABLE

G il was back. Anew. Which was something of an oxymoron, but he was back dating again, and he was a new man. The fresh *lion passant* tattoo roaring half out of his shirtsleeve announced it.

He was with a woman he met online, and they were spelunking a cave in Kentucky. Something she'd always wanted to do. Something he never wanted to do. Told him she liked her men to be "lambs at the dinner table, and lions in bed." And that's when he rolled up his sleeve the rest of the way.

She was tall and sinewy, and snaked her way easily down one of the narrow cave passages, called for him to follow. Her headlight slid across the rocks, his own light stationary as he tried to steady his breath. Tried to slow that locomotive in his chest. Keep it from jumping the tracks.

"This is great!" she said as she descended. "Now I'm glad I didn't have that extra slice of pizza. Where are you?"

"I'm here," he said. "Right behind you." Her light slowly dimmed as she eased further down, his own light fixed on that one section of rock. The drop was angled, yet seemed precipitous. A kind of anti-birth. Like entering a stony womb. *Holy hell!* he thought.

As a kid, whenever he was anxious, he'd sit in front of that small fish tank in his room. His *tropicals*. It calmed him, watching their slow, balletic meanderings. Limits negotiated with grace. Their innocuous rise of bubbles. But this. . . This was drowning in stale air. This was a monolithic straightjacket. One that *caused* madness. He adjusted his headlight, thought: *What if it failed?*

"Hey!" she called out. "Where are you?"

"I'm coming," he said, sweat dripping into his eyes. He was suffocating. Was sure of it. Her light was faintly visible now. Her voice small and distant.

"Wow," she said. "Fucking wow!"

He attempted to ease his way down the rocky slope. Felt it vice around him. Thought for a moment he couldn't see. At least not clearly. That he'd die in this passageway's rocky clutches. And she'd die too. If he couldn't get out, she couldn't get out. He wanted to think of those bygone tropicals. That bubbling tank. Find in himself some calming equivalent. But felt it was lost to him. That everything was, or soon would be.

"You can't believe what it's like down here," she said. "It opens up. It's like a grotto. Hey, you there?"

"You bet," he called to her, pressing in his shoulders and pushing himself out. His headgear scraping rock. His new self, born into his old self. His new old self. Uncorking. Gulping air. Gulping the *bigness* of air.

"Hey, what the fuck?" he barely heard her say. "I can't see your light." But he was headed for a brighter light. And bigness begot bigness. And that voice below him was getting smaller and tighter, as if the rocks themselves were speaking in a whisper. Till they didn't speak at all, and he was halfway to the mouth of the cave, with all that, whatever *that* was, behind him.

LEAPING

After my aunt left him, my uncle took to mastering sailors' knots for hours by the window facing the yard. Looking up from his intricate tangles to peer out now and then at the red bougainvillea that climbed a fence (my aunt's favorite color, always on her fingernails and lips). Still wearing that fat brown tie with a marlin leaping nearly off of it. Even when he sat, just in his boxers, he wore a dress shirt and that tie, knotted tightly.

Told wild stories of the sea, though the closest he ever got was the beach at Rockaway. Told pirate tales. Said there were even women pirates, but most people never knew that. And how sailors, seeing manatees sunning on the rocks, thought they were mermaids. "Ugly pieces of work, those manatees," he'd say. "Can you imagine the disappointment?" As I stood there with my ball and two gloves, hoping he'd take one, and we'd play catch. Back and forth in the yard like we used to: high balls and grounders, and those fast ones that nearly took your head off. Kept you on your toes.

"Watch, you'll learn something," he'd say, biting his lip, threading the rope up and over, around and through. Tugging on it when he was done, to demonstrate its reliability.

A symmetrical art he framed with his hands, hanging for a moment in his sailorman's Louvre. That marlin leaping from his chest, the bougainvillea leaping the fence in still life. The pirates leaping onto ships from that kitchen chair parked in front of the window. The baseball burning a hole in my hand. Not leaping anywhere.

SCHADENFREUDE
MAKES ME HORNY

He was playing an original composition on piano he called "Exploding Jesus." Kept banging, punching, pounding the keys (the high ones/the low ones) with very few landings between. Made it difficult for her to hear the TV—the news station she was watching—the crass politician with wild straw-blonde hair being browbeaten before a congressional committee. A politician she despised, which curled her candy apple lips as he squirmed on camera.

"Schadenfreude makes me horny," she said, turning. But he was lost, with furious fingers disassembling his threadbare longings. His musical equivalent of *God is dead*. A passion at the loss, she felt, was wasted. Felt it was better spent in wrinkling up those noisy percale sheets fresh out of the package.

When he was finished, slumped over, sweating, she said, "Did you know houseflies hum in the key of F?"

"Where do you come up with this stuff?" he said.

"Here and there," she told him, feeling sometimes that getting his attention was like diving forty feet into a tub of water.

She didn't believe in a "higher power," so she never mourned the empty spaces. Felt sad he did. Presented her one cure by ripping free the buttons of her blouse. He watched them pop one by one onto the rug. The straw-haired politician stammered behind her. It was like strumming the tigress's cage with a stick.

The Lord in fragments sailed somewhere in outer space far beyond concern. He gazed at her. And even he could hear a better music in that moment.

ROCK-A-BYE

It was an old cat hanging out of a first-floor window of an apartment building, peering down intently. I'd passed it a hundred times and it was always there, its nose against the glass as though it was trying to sniff through to the world outside. It was boney and matted and little pieces were bitten out of its ears. Its rheumy eyes would stare down at me.

As Tina and I passed below the window this time, it was open. The cat was leaning halfway out, its ears pinned back. Its paws edged toward the end of the sill.

"Shit!" Tina said. "Jeff!"

I heard myself say, "No, Kitty!"

As it leapt, I thought *cactus*, I thought *barbwire*, I thought *pain* and stepped back as the animal landed with a horrible screech and I noticed then it had only three legs. It hobbled off under a car, lowered itself and hissed. Its goopy eyes peered out at us from the shadows.

"Why didn't you catch it?" Tina snapped. "You were right there. You bastard!"

"What?"

"Look at it? It's freaked out. A leg missing and it probably just broke the other three."

"It happened so fast," I told her.

"Sure," she said. "All you ever think about is yourself."

"Not that again."

"Christ," she said. "It's old. You were right there."

I bent down snapping my fingers, said, "Kitty, kitty. Come on kitty. . ."

Tina went under the window and called up. "Hello! Hello!" She rang the bell, kept pressing the button. "Nobody's home," she said. "Shit."

"Maybe we can wait," I said.

"For what? For it to drop dead under the car?" She got down on all fours, her head street level, and began sweet-talking it. It was a voice I faintly remembered.

She took off her jacket, reached in slowly. It spat. She put her hand down in the gutter in front of it, kept it there motionless. After a bit the cat inched forward and sniffed it. She was talking to it the whole time, softly. I couldn't tell what she was saying, but eventually it came out and she wrapped it in her jacket, pressed against her breast.

As we drove to the vet, I could hear it purring. One by one she gently fingered its legs. "I don't think they're broken," she said.

"Great," I said. She turned and glared at me.

I wondered what the hell it was thinking. Was it a final fling into the wild before it went away from that sill and those drab olive curtains? What was it that Tina needed to let the past stay where it belonged? Would a handful of blood and claws have done it?

The car windows were shut and I didn't dare open them, even a crack. It was hot and I was sweating terribly, but I didn't complain. As she baby-talked, rocking it gently and rubbing the tips of its ears, the purring grew louder. Till it was finally louder than anything else.

BREAK DANCING BUTCHER

Ed's mother is dating a break dancing butcher, sixteen years her junior, she met over at Park 'N Shop. And Ed pictures his father squirming in the ground, or flinging his harp, whichever the case may be.

Over dinner (steaks), the young butcher recites a compendium of various cuts of meat as Ed squirms. Slabs you can cut with a fork. Describing animal parts like soft sculptures while Ed's mother beams, her hair in long Pocahontas braids dyed yellow. Rouge nearly in circles like an old doll.

And later, the table and chairs pushed to a corner—her legs crossed, a foot swinging to a pounding beat. She watches her meaty meat-man spinning on the kitchen floor in his T-shirt, a dragon and little devils inked into taut skin. Sweaty against the tiled floor Ed's father put in, one square at a time. His fat belly hanging over his belt. Breathing heavily one summer, and stopping often to catch his breath and take a sip of beer. His wife in rollers, a robe, asking him when the hell was she going to have her kitchen back. Telling him it was late and dinner wasn't going to cook itself.

MR. NASTY

He let her in through the garage. She was older than he'd imagined and prettier. As she hurried past, her backpack brushed his chest.

"Sorry I'm late," she said. "You got somewhere I can change?"

He took her to a small bathroom in the back he'd never got around to finishing. Above them the migrating herd of five-year-old girls thundered through the house. And the slow meandering patter of their parents could be heard, shuffling back and forth from the buffet table, and his wife of course, whizzing about with her egg-timer brain in a tizzy—her mother close behind, he was certain, soaking up every detail with her iPhone.

"Here, help me with this," the woman said, spinning around and tapping the back of her dress with a long, lacquered nail. As he drew closer, he took in the contrasting scents of perfume and perspiration. He found them equally appealing. Her makeup was heavy for the role, her hair up in a tight bun.

"You're not bashful, are you?"

"You mean like the dwarf?"

She laughed.

He put his beer bottle in his other hand and pulled down on the zipper. She wiggled her shoulders free and let the dress fall to her feet and stepped out of it. She was in her bra and panties—scooped up the dress and folded it. He turned and edged toward the door.

"Stay," she said, "while I get ready."

He tried to hide the fact that he was gawking, but did so every chance he got.

"What's the birthday girl's name?"

"Kelly," he said. But it wasn't his daughter he was thinking about. It was her mother, tearing down the stairs, ticking audibly. Wondering where the hell Snow White was.

The backyard was filled with sunlight and the kids were getting antsy. There were games to be played, a cake to light, and presents to open. Everything had to be "just so," and there was always his mother-in-law's watchful eye, monitoring each beer hissed open—the two of them tag-teaming him with that *look*. The one that said: *Get it together, you dumb shit.*

Snow White pulled a princessy gown out of her pack and he gazed now, full on, at her rear—the frilly blue panties, what filled them.

"Looks like you work out," he heard himself say, wishing he hadn't.

"How would you know *that*?" She turned, her heavily painted eyebrows arched.

"I. . ."

"Only kidding." She smiled. "I'm a gym rat. Can't get enough. Looks like you do alright yourself." She glanced over at his free weights in a corner of the next room.

"There's about three inches of dust on them," he told her.

She squeezed his bicep. "I don't think so." She pulled the gown over her head. "Here, give me some of that." She reached for the bottle and took a swig. Pulled a breath mint out of her pack and popped it.

He stared at the lipstick on the mouth of the bottle as she handed it back. It was a sight he hadn't seen in years.

She followed his eyes and tore off a sheet of toilet paper. "Let me get that," she said.

He shook his head and put the bottle to his lips and drained most of it. She slipped into a glittery pair of red pumps and put the folded dress in the pack. Grabbed a shiny black wig from another compartment and put it on, squinted into the mirror, brushing down the bangs with her hand. "So," she said, looking at him in the mirror. "If you're not Bashful, which one are you?"

The migrating wildebeests rumbled down the hall and he heard what sounded like a bowling ball dropped. "You mean the Seven Dwarfs?"

"Or the eighth, if you like." Her face brightened.

Nasty, he thought. *I'd be Mr. Nasty.* "Let me think about it," he told her.

"Don't take *too* long," she said. "That little cottage in the woods is getting pretty crowded." She handed him a card over her shoulder without turning. "I don't only work with kids. I do private parties too." She caught his eye in the mirror and gave him a look that wouldn't quit. He put the card in his pocket. It was not the cartoony one his wife had pressed against the fridge with a bunny magnet.

"I'd better go up the front way," she said. "A princess must always maintain her dignity." He imagined some of the other costumes she had in her collection. She was a shapeshifter, right now out of Disney. But he could still feel her inside—another character altogether.

"I'd be Mr. Na..." he began. But he couldn't get it out. "What?"

"Forget it," he told her, thinking how seventeen years of marriage can give you lockjaw sometimes. He pulled back the beer and emptied it, opened the garage door and listened to it rattle up. Then Snow White glided up the steps and rang the bell.

A RUSH OF SHADOWS

She fell in with some bad nuns who smoked pot behind the rectory. The eldest had a past, a prison tattoo: the name *Emma* in a heart cracked down the middle under her robes. The other stuttered, and cursed herself for doing so. Said the high point of her life was going up all those stairs in the Statue of Liberty as a kid, and looking out from the big lady's crown. Her little eyes above those big ones. Both heads in the clouds.

After a jet made a gray scar above them and it was quiet again, the nun with the tattoo said, "Inexhaustible abundance is a myth. You'd be wise to remember that." The novice nodded—watched some fast-moving clouds send a rush of shadows across a half-painted house in the distance. Wondered who the hell Emma was.

THE CLEANING GIRL

It was great having the house to herself. That big, fancy house. She went into the cow's bedroom and sat down on the edge of the bed. It had a memory foam topper and she pressed her hand into it, was endlessly amused watching the imprint vanish. Now that the bed was stripped, she was looking forward to pressing her whole body into it.

The cow's husband was on the dresser beside her, and there were those tricky eyes of his that were always on her when the cow wasn't looking. When he'd smile and she'd smile back.

She got up and went through the top drawer where the jewelry was kept—all that glitter wasted. What, after all, did a cow need with jewelry? She put the necklaces on first, the pearls, the gold chains, the teardrop diamonds. Then the rings, which kept slipping off. So she held her hands up as though she were drying her nails, finally deciding to put the rings on her thumbs.

She took one of the special bras from a drawer, red and lacy—new-looking like it had never been worn—and put it on over her small breasts. She took several of the husband's socks and stuffed each cup. It felt good having something of his against her. She looked in the mirror, shifted her weight from one foot to the other, tilted her head, smiled coyly. He'd like that, she thought. She twisted out some lipstick, *Berry Burst*, and painted her lips, breaching the edges and getting some on her teeth.

She brushed her long hair down over one eye and peeked out through it, the room appealingly striated. She was reaching for some bracelets when the doorbell rang. She froze for a moment as though the stillness might make her invisible. Then she pictured the cow at the door with an armload of packages. She scrambled in a panic. It rang again. She broke for the kitchen and grabbed her coat, buttoned it up tight. *The rings!* She slid them off and into her pockets.

Not only would she be fired, she'd probably be arrested. Even though she hadn't intended to steal anything. But what would that matter. The cow would see to it that it wouldn't matter. She'd say she had a chill when she was questioned about the coat. She was sick and needed to go home. She'd put the jewelry back when she could. She hurried to the door and opened it.

There was a small package on the top step and a UPS truck pulling away.

She brought it in, swung the door shut and bolted to the bedroom, slipping off the necklaces as she did. She put everything back and sat on the edge of the bed with the coat on her lap, panting. Decided she'd keep the lipstick on, right where it belonged. The cow and the gawker looked at her from a gilded frame. She gave them both the finger.

SUPERHERO

I do not have a superpower. But an uncanny ability to finish sentences. This, of course, does not translate to crime fighting—swinging from a spidery thread up or down a skyscraper. But flinging, instead, the populace at the Peaceful Willow Rest Home into a state of awe and wonder. Prying loose pieces of syntax from the rubble. The names of favorite shows and presidents, trapped in walls, particles of plaster trickling down as their aging minds strain to think.

"Tapioca," I tell Mrs. Green, trying to describe what otherwise translates, descriptively, as "mud." Nobody's thinking I'm a bird, a plane, faster than a speeding bullet. Yet I see through walls.

"Your uncle, Jake," I say to another. "The tall one with the nice smile. That who?" And: "You mean Rose Sunset? That pretty rouge you wear? Tyrone Power. . . Epsom salts. . . Chrysanthemums. . ." I say. "You're certainly welcome. Close," I say. "But it's Roy. Oh, hon," I say, "think nothing of it."

THE SURROGATE

Butterflies kept landing on her, the surrogate told them. The older couple. Older, as in their late thirties. The husband's harvested sperm growing inside her. Ballooning her out, as she leaned back in the lawn chair and they stood there with bags of food and vitamins.

Maybe you were a rhododendron in another life, the husband said.

What? She peered at him through heart-shaped sunglasses with red glitter around the rims. Pulled up some kind of drink to her darkly painted lips. They watched it (whatever it was) go down.

The butterflies landing on you, he said.

Oh—yeah. It's supposed to be good luck. There was a tabloid spread open on her lap. An owl-eyed alien creature stared up at them. They felt she was thinner than they'd like. Hoped she wasn't doing drugs. *A bird pooped on me the other day,* the girl said. *What would that make me in another life? A statue?*

The couple laughed. For too long and too loudly. Then the wife stepped forward and stood over the girl, smiling queerly. Shook a bottle of multivitamins at her like a shaman's rattle, inches from her face.

FLATWARE

I was eating from a carton of Chinese takeout, with half a load on, when I heard someone come in through the sliding door in the back. I hid behind the wall and when I saw him turn toward the kitchen, I plunged my fork in his neck.

He stood there with his jaw swung open and his eyes bugged out looking at me—the fork moving up and down as he yelled, "What the fuck?" A trickle of blood darkened his collar. "You idiot! You stabbed me!" he screeched.

Damn! I thought, as it came to me. He looked like my neighbor, Bill—sort of. *Damn, damn, damn.*

He reached for the fork and I shouted, "No!—don't touch that. It might really start bleeding if you pull it out."

"It hurts like a sonofabitch."

"You're Bill's brother."

"No shit," he said. "My nephew knocked his ball over your fence."

"Christ. I'm sorry. I thought. . ."

"Screw what you thought. Call 911!"

"I'll drive you," I told him. "It'll be quicker."

As I tore through traffic, I saw him looking in the visor mirror, holding the end of the fork and grumbling to himself.

I wondered if there was Kung Pao chicken coursing through an artery—hoping there wasn't one of those little red pepper chips I loved so much on the end of the fork.

At the ER they rushed him through, and I tagged along sheepishly. The attending swooped in with a gaggle of residents in tow, but it turned out the fork didn't hit anything vital, mostly muscle, and he didn't even need a stitch. But they gave him a shot, and gave me "a look" when they heard the story. And I thought for a minute they might call the law on me. But he insisted it was an accident and they let it drop.

On the way back we talked—mainly me saying what a dumb shit I was for not giving him a chance to explain before letting him have it. I could tell he'd feel a lot better if he could just toss me out the window on the freeway. He was a pretty big guy and I remember Bill mentioning his younger brother—the football star in high school that got all the babes and even played a bit in college.

I shook his hand when we got out of the car, and I felt my fingers crunch. A small payback perhaps, for the neck jewelry I contributed so freely. Bill and his wife and three kids came out and it all was explained. Everyone staring at the large bandage covering one side of his neck—at the little red dots at the center of it. Then the group, as one, turned toward me, glowering.

I went back in and sat in the kitchen, wondering if I should call Tina at her sister's, where she always went after one of our big blow-outs. Decided she considered me a gigantic asshole as it was, and this would move me to a *black hole in space* status I'd be better off without. I'd lost my appetite by then, thinking of that look on Bill's brother's face when I asked the doctor for the fork back. It was a favorite from a set Tina and I got as a wedding present. I put it in the sink and ran some hot water over it. I pulled a beer from a six pack and figured I'd be doing some serious damage to the other five.

Later that night, I went out in the yard with a flashlight and found the ball under some Sweet Williams my wife was always fussing over, worse for wear since she'd been gone. It was quiet. It was very late. I tossed the ball over the fence and listened for its soft thump as it landed.

BAD-BOY WANNABE AND THE CEPHALOPOD EMPIRE

It was late, and I was more than a little drunk when my face blew off and landed in the river. We were smoking a joint and the fish, or what looked like a fish, laughed as we saw it drift off under the bridge.

We'd just left the party for some air and a few lungfuls of weed. We were strangers who had one dance together and then the joint came out. She held it up like an exclamation point to something not needing to be spoken.

Her fish mask was on top of her head now with the elastic band under her chin. "I'm a cephalopod, if you're wondering," she said. I was.

"A who-the-what?" I said.

"A squid, basically," she said. "They rock. This stupid mask was as close as I could get." She took a long pull of smoke and passed the joint.

"I never thought much about squids," I told her, thinking this was a first: my devil mask, with the bad-boy forked tongue curling out, was floating down the river and I was talking with a squid. A squid that apparently knew at least one big word. I was, at best, a bad-boy wannabe, and the mask ripped off by a bit of wind seemed fitting. I was myself now. The bridge lights were becoming a smeary yellow as the pot made its way to all those brain centers it was kicking down the doors to. "What makes them so special?"

"Are you kidding?" she said. "Before there were dinosaurs, before there were fish even, there were cephalopods. Hey, they invented the act of swimming."

"Wow," I said, feeling stupid, wishing I had my devil mask back on. "Wow" was not one half of a conversation. I passed over the joint (what was left of it) wishing never to see it again.

"We think we're so special," she said, "with all our *things*. Who needs all that crap? But animals, they got it going on. Before we crawled out of the sea, we had these babies to thank." She tapped the plastic fish face on her head.

I'd just gotten a pricey car, with the scent of new leather, I wanted to show off. But now I was feeling bad for not having a proclivity for jet propulsion, or a clever fishy quip that might let her know I had a brain up there somewhere.

"That's fascinating," I said, waving off the last small fire she was offering. I thought to go down to the bank on the other side of the bridge to see if the mask had, perhaps, landed up against it. There was an aardvark and a something else with curled horns walking toward us. The aardvark was laughing so loudly it spilled most of its drink, making it laugh even louder. The animal kingdom, I thought. Fish, I thought. Super fish, I thought. Squinting in the dim light, I noticed for the first time she hadn't any makeup on. And how pretty she was without it. I wanted to kiss her, but moments swim away too quickly sometimes, and are far too slippery to recapture.

I watched her mask slip back down and we stood. I wanted to say, "Wait!" But what for? She was a cephalopod after all, and I couldn't keep up. The band was playing a song I didn't know the name of, but never liked. I thought to turn and climb down toward the river, but headed back to the party, in her wake, instead.

LION'S HEAD MEATBALLS

Mom was making Lion's Head meatballs, which actually looked somewhat like lions' heads (her personal touch)—sculptured just so. I was helping, but mine were lumpy and featureless. Hers would be roaring up at my father soon enough.

She caught him eye-fucking her younger sister earlier that day, and no matter how he denied it, she was on him like a bucket of Crazy Glue.

"I should have given you a towel so you could wipe the drool off," she said.

"You got nothing better to do?" my father said. "You gotta torment me for doing nothing."

"I'll give you *nothing*," she said. "I know *something* when I see it." He waved her off and turned on the TV, plopped down in his overstuffed chair.

"You wanna watch the game?" he asked me. I could never get enough of the Yankees back then, but looked up at my mother for permission.

"Go," she said, and I placed my latest malformed effort with the other meatballs.

"Don't forget to close your eyes when the commercials come on," my father told me. "You never know what you might be accused of."

"Cute," my mother said. "Teach him disrespect. God, I thought your eyes were gonna pop out and roll down your chest."

Mantle was up and I could tell my father wasn't really paying attention. Mantle had a great home run streak going, but the dirty-look spears my mother was flinging were distracting. My father looked at me and swung his head toward the fridge, and I knew what that meant. I got a beer and punched two holes in the can. He went out the window with it onto the fire escape, curled a finger my way, and I joined him.

The game and the crowd followed in tow. It was like listening to the radio now. My father shook his head, offered me a swallow. I took it. Made a face.

"They're different," he told me, pointing this time with a protruding thumb. "I wish I could teach you something that would help. But you'll have to suffer it on your own."

"Moms?" I said.

"Women," he said. "They're not like us."

I didn't know what to do with that. He didn't know what more to do with it either, so we just stared off at a flock of homing pigeons leaving a roof, churning the sky as one. We listened to the TV-radio and said, "Yes!" in unison when something good happened for the home team. I couldn't know, of course, it would only be a few short years before he'd leave us, and nothing would ever be the same.

The Lion's Head meatballs were delicious. But a little scary too.

BUG PORN

Curled over the microscope, he was watching cells divide in a harsh moon of light. *What are you up to?* she asked. She had come down the short flight of stairs, wearing a lacy red bra over her blouse. Just to be silly. To see where it might go.

Watching bug porn, he said, with one eye squinted shut. When he opened it and looked at her, he shook his head. Jotted something in a notebook. They were in the basement, where he had his office, and she noticed a daddy longlegs above them on the low ceiling. Thought how stunningly elegant it was, that tiny body ambling on slender threads. When she pointed it out, he stood quickly and swung his notebook, smashing it just inches from the light bulb.

Bug porn, she said after a pause, and could see he was pleased that she had registered his little joke. She reached back and unhooked her bra. Flung it over her shoulder, a dangling epaulet. Gazed up at the single leg stuck to the ceiling. Angled, just so, like a forward slash. With all of the surrounding grammar missing.

WATERFALL IN STILL LIFE

She tore up the lottery tickets and scattered them out the window, a sad confetti for the parade of things that could have been.

Her son sat on the couch with his bags packed. He was going where the weather was cold and unforgiving. Where he and a group of friends would attempt to ice climb a frozen waterfall. She came over and sat across from him in her recliner.

"Can you imagine," he said, "a frozen waterfall, all that gushing water frozen solid?"

"You be careful," she said.

"Of course. I'm stoked."

"You're what?"

"Excited."

"I'll miss you," she said.

"I'll write," he told her. "Send pictures. I'll call."

They were surrounded by her bobblehead doll collection. Thirty-plus years' worth. Sometimes they creeped him out. They were everywhere. Their heads on springs: animals, celebrities, sports figures, cartoon characters, politicians, superheroes. . .

She wished his father were here to see him so strapping and full of adventure like he was when *they* were young. She lit a cigarette.

"Those things. . ." he began.

But she held up a hand like a traffic cop. She had a small stack of lottery tickets left on the end table beside her. She caught his eyes landing on them. "There's a million bucks in there waiting. It'll give me something to do later."

"You bet," he said. "Maybe more."

She took a puff, tapped some ash in her hand. He reached for an ashtray, but she waved him off. "You've got guts," she said. "Like your old man. He was brave too. I could tell you stories. . ."

He smiled, looked at his watch. "I'm gonna call Uber," he said. He gave her a droopy, apologetic look. One she'd seen a lot from him lately.

"I'm fine," she said. "My shows are on later. And your sister's calling. You know how she can chew your ear off. You stay warm. Hear? A frozen waterfall," she said. "Whoever heard of such a thing?"

He went over and hugged her. "I'm calling," he said and took out his phone. "They'll be here in four minutes." He put his bags and backpack by the door.

She got up and they hugged again, her one arm at her side, the cigarette smoke curling up. Five minutes later he was out the door. But she wasn't alone. One by one she went around the room tapping the head of each doll till they all wobbled and bobbled and nodded in unison. She sat in the recliner, their nucleus, and soaked up the stillness-defying energy. She put out her cigarette in the ashtray and reached for the TV remote.

She shook her own head, in contrast, from side to side. Thought: water just wasn't supposed to behave like that. No way, no how.

THE PENCIL

He's hiding in the restroom stall, his feet up on the seat. He's hiding as much as anyone can in a stall with the top and the bottom open. There are other students in the restroom, some speaking, sotto voce, into phones. Others with shaky voices whispering: "Shh. . ." There is screaming in the halls and gunfire, even pleading, more gunfire. . .

When the door bursts open there is a shriek from the stall beside him. A boot pounding against that stall door. Then Emily whimpering, crawling under the open space between them. Her frail frame rising in front of him with her hand over her mouth, shaking.

The door-battering stops. And the boy knows the shooter will see her legs and his stall will be next. When her hand drops he sees that she is moving her lips with little sound coming out and realizes she is praying. He puts his arms around her and then he spots the muzzle tip lowered under the door and shouts. The shots are loud. She buckles with her legs horrible ounces heavier. She drops. More shots.

Two stall doors swing open and the boy hears the sound of frantic footsteps race out into the hall. Then the boot against his door, hard adrenalin-rich pounding, grunts, till the lock gives and the shooter pushes past the body on the floor and crazed eyes, Andrew's crazed eyes, are upon him. The boy is on the seat with legs up, bent like a frog, and the rifle is in his face.

"Jenkins?" the shooter says. "What the fuck? You praying?"

The boy shakes his head that he isn't. The boy wants to say something. Some last something like "No!" or "Please!" But his lips are trembling and his breath is corked, wordless.

"No worries," the shooter says. "We're good. That pencil you let me borrow in homeroom—the one with your teeth marks in it—we're good."

The boy nods. He wants his body to stop shaking, thinks somehow that trembling might excite that muzzle, what is behind it. But there are no commands he knows of that will make it so. The muzzle, the shooter turn then. Head back out into the hall. The boy looks down. Emily's eyes are open, looking nowhere. He tries to stand, and slips.

A faucet is running. Through the screaming and the return fire now, he can hear a faucet running. Clearly. The gush of it. How normal a thing. How strange.

MECHANICS

The scent of all those miles was in his clothes. The grease and oil and tire rubber. The car parts rubbed off into him. Close as she'd get to those road trips they never took. His thick arm around her on the couch as they watched their shows. Teaching her how to blow smoke rings during the commercials. All those O's wiggling off into oblivion.

Yellow was her favorite color and she was wearing banana earrings. Two small porcelain bunches. He liked to flick at them now and then to tease her. When a wispy, malformed circle pushed from her lips, he said, "Good. Now do a 'W.' Then you can spell WOW." She slapped him playfully on the shoulder, went back to blowing the smoke out in the smooth streams to which she was accustomed.

A fly came in the open window and landed on one of the figurines she got when her mother died. Thirty-plus years' worth, everywhere throughout their apartment. A particular one of a girl in a puffy white dress holding a basket of fruit. The fly was on the little girl's bonnet. All those little girls her mom collected, so unlike the one she had. The fly made a more fitting hat, she thought, as the last few circles of his smoke came apart and vanished. Leaving behind only the smell of them. The vaguest proof they were ever there in any form at all.

OUCH! (A LOVE STORY)

For the hell of it he searches the web for "quirky" porn and sees his wife in bed with a clown (actually they are on a haystack). It is *her* alright, thirty-ish years younger. He has seen photos of her at that age. It's Abby, he thinks, in some sleazeball film about the Big Top called *Clownin' Around*. He clicks it off. Reflects on time's often cruel diminishments. A bit like Russian nesting dolls. Each one inside the other—when removed—a smaller version of the one that preceded it.

On Saturdays he volunteers at a local old folks' home. Reads from a book of poems to an elderly blind woman who sits in a lawn chair out back. When he gets to a poem by Margaret Atwood, she has him reread the same stanza repeatedly, as she sips her tea and turns dead eyes inward.

"I would like to be the air
that inhabits you for a moment
only. I would like to be that unnoticed
& that necessary."

They met as colleagues working at the campus library. *Imbroglio* was only in some of the books that surrounded them, never a component in their lives together that followed. The closest they came was when he rehearsed lines with her for an acting class she took. That deep and dark voice unlike his own. A character he played. The sex that night, the better for it.

They have a serious ant problem. Columns of black marauders roam from unseen places. Up and down the walls. He suggests they call an exterminator. But she says she can handle it/ they can handle it. She carpet-bombs the trails with quick bursts of Windex. "The ammonia," she says, darting about in an active blur. The ants trickle down in bubbly ruin. Float on fumy rivers. "Have at it," she says, holding out the spray bottle. When he takes it, she brightens. He pursues each determined column with demonstrative focus—with a big game hunter's aim and intention. She scans the walls, then grabs back the bottle, and as he points here and there and she responds so eagerly, so robustly, he feels like the air that inhabits her for a moment. That unnoticed. That necessary.

A PENCHANT
FOR RENEGADES

With a penchant for renegades, Beth dated a Mexican wrestler who wore a scary mask. Knew a lot about birds.

Said, when she was more interested in sex than facts: "There's a bird that uses farts to make worms come out of the ground."

Said: "A mockingbird can copy many sounds. Even dogs. Machines too."

Said: "There's a seagull that hunts whales. Swoops down and takes bites out of them."

Said: "There's a bird that drops a bug in the water, then eats the fish that eats the bug." He stopped to sip his beer.

"Wear the mask again," Beth said.

OVEN GLOVES

Walter was still wearing the rubber antlers from the Christmas party. His Rudolf the Reindeer red nose, which was really a rubber clown nose, lay between the salt and pepper shakers. It was late and the old diner waitress kept calling him Bullwinkle (the goofy cartoon moose from his childhood) each time she filled his coffee cup.

His Snow Queen wife of twenty-seven years glittered across from him. "I pitched it," Walter said. "Hard. But all he could do was say 'Uh huh, uh huh,' and eyeball that bimbo in the elf outfit shaking her butt all over the place. What elf is six one in heels? *Christ.*"

She laid down her wand and slipped out of her coat. "How about a steak?" she said. "A nice juicy one?"

"They got antacids on the menu? I could use a soup bowl full."

"Maybe you're shooting too high," she said. "Aim a little lower, you'll hit."

"I've been shooting into the dirt my whole life. Wearing oven gloves for everything I touch." His glasses fogged with steam as he sipped.

"Cooking metaphors suit you," she said and smiled.

"What's that supposed to mean?" She shrugged and a bit of glitter sprinkled onto the seat.

"My goose is cooked with this company," he said. "How's that for a cooking metaphor?"

She reached a gloved hand across the table, grazing the clown nose. She had offered to get him one she'd seen that flickered on and off, but he said the clown nose was good enough.

The gloves were white and she'd meticulously sewn sequins to the backs of them. Outside the plate glass, snow was beginning to dust the fat backs of cars. A cat ran under one of them. It was black and she found the contrast stunning. The waitress came over and filled her cup, then his.

"Here ya go Bullwinkle," she said. And without looking up, he thanked her.

DEATH'S LATE-NIGHT WALKS

Three times a week he walked his dog in the Grim Reaper costume he'd kept from two Halloweens ago. It was at night and the kids—*the rowdies*, he called them—smoking pot and drinking on a stone bench in the children's playground, didn't know what to make of the black hood or the scythe. Especially the scythe. His Chihuahua barked at them each time he passed, donning that little red sweater Death's wife knitted for it. And the man never responded, just bent with his hand in a sandwich bag whenever the dog pooped and said, *Good boy, Clarence,* in a little voice from out of the darkness of that peaked black hood, for only the dog to hear.

A DISADVANTAGE
OF MOMENTUM

Phil sat on the edge of the bed in the ER as Nan vacuously leafed through a dog-eared magazine. He pulled back his hospital gown and slowly lifted the ice pack molded around his penis.

"Is it still bleeding?"

"Not much anymore," he said.

"Hell," she said and he nodded.

He rocked his legs back and forth, nearly banging his knees together. It was a habit she never liked. The merest bit of anxiousness and they were off to the races, those legs. She'd feel them in overdrive under the table when a waiter wasn't quick enough with a menu. Or at an auditorium, with one or the other of their kids on stage when they were little. It didn't matter who was sitting beside him or how many looks she gave him.

"Maybe you should slow it down a bit."

"Do what?"

"Your legs," she said. "Gets the circulation going."

"You know how I hate waiting."

"It's a good sign. If it was serious, they'd be right on it."

"Now there's a thought," he said and Nan laughed. She

put her hand on his knee and the rocking slowed. He looked again. Nan's teeth marks were on either side, in deep.

"Quit fussing with it. You'll get it going again."

With the last kid gone, they'd been rattling around the big house getting bigger all the time. Now there were only the weekly couples sessions with Heidi in that small office with a fish tank, and a framed nature print over each of their heads.

"Spice it up," she'd encouraged. "Be creative—now's the time."

So Nan went along with one of Phil's adolescent fantasies, and went down on him as he drove home from Chow Ling's in heavy traffic. When he threw his head back and yelled out something that seemed in another language, they banged into the car in front of them. It was just a fender bender at a stoplight, but the words that followed were in a language she understood. She rose up from the collapsing airbag, shaken. Took a quick look, then scrambled out of the vehicle apologizing and exchanging insurance information with the other driver. Phil waited in the car with a firm grip on what mattered.

Then it was off to the ER, the two of them red-faced as they were triaged, Phil's hand sheepishly down the front of his pants.

Nan stood up and brushed some long comb-over stragglers from his eyes.

"It just struck me," she said, "that if anyone wanted to buy you a Get Well card, they'd have to go to one of those sex shops." He smiled.

She looked down and touched him where his hand lay under his gown. "Anything left?" she asked.

"Enough," he said, after a pause, wondering if she was referring to the big picture or it was just her attempt at a bit of humor—figured he'd cover both bases.

They heard some laughter and watched as shadows gathered behind the curtain, grew. Then a hand reached in and swung it open.

WHAT REMAINS

She tells me she saw shadows on the wall. What looked like robots in top hats. She's been hitting the morphine pump pretty good. Says watching that small TV is like looking at a rock in a snowstorm. And would I tap some salt on her tongue. Those packets. She wants to feel the tang. *Something. Anything other...* That tongue that taught English Lit to troubled teens. Hemingway's big fish in ruin. The catcher in that chest-high rye, catching. A tongue that wags at nurses flying by. "Now the sugar," she says. Points. Sticks her tongue out at me again.

BROKEN TALE

It was a long time ago and we were young. Lived in a tiny flat across from some batshit crazy bikers. Annie worked the phones at Suicide Prevention. Would come home dog-eared and weighted down. She'd kick off her shoes, and I'd rub her feet.

I sold little bags of marijuana to pay the bills and wrote poetry to keep my head from exploding. There were days when getting the words right was like trying to squeeze a rock and hoping it would play music. That's when I sold more/smoked more.

Annie's head was stuffed with all those disparate voices. You could feel how swollen it was. She'd smoke a joint and I'd hit those delicate pressure points and she'd cry out, let me know, *That was a good one!* We had a cat with a broken tail and it would jump up on the couch with us and purr. There were a lot of broken things. But we didn't know it then. And that got us through.

She'd tell me all the stories that seeped into those little holes in the phone to the bigger one in her head, and slowly her head would get back to normal. The bikers revved their Harleys across the way, drunk on the notion there were those mechanical beasts under their nuts. The cat jumped down when we made love. The motorcycles drowned us out.

I recall one story she told me, that haunted us both, of a mother (stoned on PCP) who nearly boiled her infant in a bubbling stew pot. Some thread of sanity stopping her in time. And that's when she called. How Annie talked her down afterward, barely able to breathe. She didn't want a foot massage that night. The cat sat between us, swishing its boomerang-shaped tail as if it knew something was up. We didn't speak. Stuck our heads, instead, into that 13" black-and-white TV we had back then. *Way* too snug. How nevertheless, we made them fit.

ONLY THAT

At the nude lake he told her, if she was breaking up with him, then he'd just have to drown himself in the fucking lake. She was petting a German Shepherd with a red bandana around its neck, and a name tag that said Dylan. A moment earlier the dog had sprinkled them with lake water. He cringed, said, "Fuck!" She patted its rump.

"I'm done," she told him. Only that. Scratched the animal behind the ear.

"I'm not bluffing," he said and headed for the water. Stirred up silt as he entered—slime-dark and murky. He always felt there were teeth lurking in silt. Pincers and fangs. Some things never changed. He swam out to the center of the lake and treaded there for a moment, looking at her looking back at him. Then he went under. A yellow lab, he could see its legs paddling, passed nearby. He wondered how long he could stay under. If his lungs might give out and he'd drown for real. If she'd swim out to him, screaming to others, perhaps closer, to rescue him. The pressure was building and his eyes bulged and his cheeks bulged, but he continued swimming down, letting air out a little at a time to keep himself from rising. He was determined. The trapped air remaining banged at his lips to escape. Maybe he'd even open his mouth and fill his lungs like a couple of balloons. He pictured her weeping on shore, banging her fists against the sides of her head. The police boats trawling with their hooks, the divers. Christ, the divers in those black wet suits. He let the few remaining bubbles bully their way out and surged to the surface, gasping like an unhooked fish.

She was still petting the dog, which was lying on their blanket now. A tall man with a beard on the other side of it, petting the dog also. The dog's eyes were slits, or at least, that's how he imagined them. She and the bearded man seemed to be chatting, occasionally laughing. The man had apparently brought over a large radio and he couldn't be sure, but he thought he heard rap music playing. He hated rap. The yellow lab he'd seen earlier in the water circled and drew close with a ball in its mouth, its eyes eager. "Fuck off," he said and swam back in.

WATERING HOLE

It was a country bar outside of town. A place where you could shoot-the-shit with the barkeep between his rag swipes sopping up the wet circles, or just watch TV without someone nagging in a language they were determined to unlearn.

In the small bathroom, there was a broken condom dispenser, duct taped shut, and part of an old fun house mirror over the sink. One that made you pie-faced, and undulated when you peered into it. Put there for a laugh, but also with the hope nobody'd notice how watered down the drinks were.

THE HORNS

He said he was a rodeo clown, and it was harder than it looked. Sometimes you had to climb inside a barrel to keep from getting the horns. "But life ain't like that." He took in another shot of whisky as though it was a last breath.

"Like what?" she said.

"Barrels to hide in. You get the horns."

She turned to her own drink, then up at the TV high above the cathedral of booze bottles. A guy was throwing a ball and another guy was catching it. A third stood over the catcher's shoulder and gauged where it stopped. Her feet were killing her. All day at the dollar store ringing up crap. Felt like they were puffing out of her shoes. Some tough guy, she thought. Even the best of them were little boys inside, lookin' for a mommy to put a Band-Aid on something or other.

"It's what you make it," she heard herself say, crossing her legs and letting a high heel dangle from her toes. He stared down from over his drink for a moment, then said, "Bullshit."

"Let's not bring up work," she said, and he smiled. A lopsided, tough-guy grin. And she wondered how deep the horns were in. Hoped he had a nice place. But was long past being picky. She put her hand on his knee and he seemed to like that. Hell, she had a purse full of Band-Aids and a night full of time.

The three guys on the TV were still at it. Throwing, catching, and looking down at the ball like its sudden appearance was a big surprise. She wondered if the one with the big stick was actually going to do something worth doing. Or just stand there.

HIS INK AND
MISS ATOMIC BOMB
(IN TRIPTYCH)

I

All his stories, he said, were written in his ink. There was even a tattoo under his full head of hair she'd never seen, but glimpsed the shadow of. She fingered the ones on his chest and thought it peculiar and amusing how some curly black hairs poked through them in the oddest places.

II

Her great aunt was Miss Atomic Bomb in the 1950s. She showed him a photo of her in a bathing suit, young and beautiful—a mushroom cloud crown on her head, a bunch of grinning soldiers gathered around. Said how she died at ninety—left behind over a hundred Chia Pets. The withered plant life browning in their decorative planters her family dumped. No real pets. She imagined Miss Atomic Bomb as a tattoo added to his picture book body, had it been *his* aunt. Ever young—flourishing for as long as he did.

III

In the diner, she couldn't help staring at the creature clawing out of his collar, cinched by a dark tie cutting into his neck.

Wore it for a job interview he was back from. She wondered what its story was, and the prison ones too. The crude spook-show tats, shiny when he got out of the shower. When he took her and she was among them. Their thicket. Unlike her husband's blank canvas.

Across from her on one hand: LOVE. On the other: HATE. A letter for each knuckle. LOVE holding the fork. HATE cutting into his pancakes.

SOLILOQUY

My uncle told me many things that last week in the ward.

He said: "Regret is a sharpshooter. No need to provide the bullets."

He said: "Loss is a short-order cook with a flair for flambé. But the flames die down, eventually."

He said: "A light fixture dropping on your head should not be confused with enlightenment."

He said: "You don't need to collect coffin lids to make yourself feel more alive. Just put your shoes on in the morning and let them do their job."

He said: "Now give me some more of that crushed ice like a good boy, will ya?"

LITTLE CASTLES

If a snowman could take a crap, that's what it would look like," he said, referring to the Pomeranian puppy a woman was walking across the street. He was saying stuff like that more and more lately, she thought. Needing, it seemed, to build his little castles on someone else's ashes.

His pit bull panted in front of him in its harness. He had his shirt open, with nothing on beneath it, and she considered the tattoos that covered so much of him, a kind of costume now. One she would have been taken with earlier in her life. But that notion had long since rusted out like many of the car parts scattered in his yard.

He'd fixed her Volvo, and seemed decent enough at the time. They'd been seeing each other for several months since. But during this walk, she was set on ending things. He'd told her he was considering having her name tattooed on one of the few sections of "canvas" left, high up on his shoulder. She urged him not to. They were on his deck at the time, and when a butterfly landed on him—and she was about to say, "Don't move"—he smashed it. Later, he said, "What's with the look?"

A Rottweiler approached them, taut on a leash, pulling along a short, muscular man with mirrored sunglasses. It stood over his pit, stared down at it. The pit rolled on its back with its legs spread apart. The Rottweiler sniffed it and stood there for a moment, as if it were considering something, then moved on. The pit scrambled back up.

"Kong!" he chided. Was quiet after that, and she noticed a look, just under his more familiar, pissed off one. Something in the eyes that a skier might have, trying to outrun an avalanche. And determined it the perfect time to tell him.

FUN HOUSE

She'd gotten the fun house mirrors at an auction and had them put up in the spare bedroom. He found them strange, even a little disturbing, and thought the buy extravagant with the kids away at college and the big tuition bucks spilling out. But she'd insisted on a "well-deserved splurge" after all that *straight and narrow*. A side of her new to him.

So he went along. Even following her one night, with a bottle of Marques de Riscal, into that room with the lights dimmed and candles she placed on both dressers, adding to the mix. In bed, she began taking off her clothes, then his. "No way," he said, draining the last of the wine, gazing into one of the mirrors overhead, at their stretched-out, undulating forms: fleshy waves of them in the sheets.

He started to sit up, but she pulled him back. "This is weird, Connie," he said.

She reached out a zigzaggy hand and ran it down his zigzaggy middle. Looking left, she was squat and condensed, her cheeks bulged as if she had two small apples stuffed in her mouth—her breasts large, wobbly globes. She guided his hand to them.

In another, the two of them were amoeboid, transforming silvery strangers. "You've got to be kidding me," he said. She smiled. And at a glance it was an astonishingly wide curl, liquid as mercury. He continued shifting his vision.

"My God!" he said.

"What?"

"The size of that thing."

She leaned over and whispered something. A name, he thought—not his own. Perhaps an endearment. She shook out her hair—jagged bolts against his chest. He closed his eyes, and when he opened them she was wriggly and rosy. A stick figure, a block, a fleshy smear—strange and elegant. He heard some low, guttural sounds—his own.

She bit his shoulder and he pulled her close. His eyes banged against each corner of their sockets. The room was cluttered. It was ablaze with candlelight—squat fiery balls, elongated licks of light, and all their odd and flagrant infidelities in every piece of glass.

FAKE EUNUCH

He'd been The Mad Magician, but his knees went out on him, so now he was doing low-budget porn. As The Mad Magician, he had a following. Did this thing in the ring where he blew a neon green powder into an opponent's face, causing them to waver helplessly in a glaze-eyed stupor. A few well-choreographed blows, and he'd have them pinned to the mat, soaking up boos from the crowd with a villain's privilege. But his knees went bad, and now it was still his bulk (particularly placed) that was keeping him gainfully employed.

The director was a woman, and she had him dressed in ancient Arabian garb, holding a long curved sword. Told him that he'd be playing a eunuch guarding a harem, but that he was only *pretending* to be a eunuch, and that he was a greedy bastard and would be getting it on with all of them. That it would be targeted for women. And that women liked a little story with their smut. He listened, nodded, thought if he could be The Mad Magician, he could be The Fake Eunuch. He just hoped his knees would hold out, and the pain wouldn't take the starch out.

She introduced him to the harem, and they smiled. One of them squeezed his bicep. Another straightened his turban and said she liked his tattoos. His stage name was Rod Bigg, but his real name was Clarence Goode. He downed another pain pill when the director wasn't looking, and reminded himself not to gaze too long into the lights. The fair maidens were sprawled out on huge pillows purchased at Walmart. The sultan would be called off, and his horny bevy would grumble at the loss. Not Shakespeare, he thought.

"Okay," said the director, "that's where you come in. Hope you've been eating your Wheaties." She gave him a slap on the butt, and had the cameraman move in.

He considered his kids, the alimony payments, his apartment, and all those TV dinners and booze that weren't getting any cheaper. He tilted his turban back the way it was. Thought, if his knees held out, even a little, he had a chance.

ERASING THE DISTANCE

He heard the ninety-year-old woman he was strapped to shout what sounded like "Woo-hoo!" Something an excited teenager might yell, as they quickly erased the distance between themselves and the earth they hurtled toward in freefall.

Moments earlier in the plane, she'd flirted with him. A small bag of bones with every follicle of her hair missing, even her eyebrows. "If I were only seventy years younger," she said, winking. They fitted up, and she said, "Hubba, hubba," as their bodies were fastened together. It was her birthday, and this was the gift her kids and grandkids had given her. What she'd insisted on doing.

He could tell by her movements she was in great pain, but she never complained. Only once taking a pill and sip of water. Smiling big as the sky they would enter.

Her voice shot past him, and he wasn't entirely sure but thought it was "Woo-hoo!" Wanted it to be, as her arms waved wildly, then stretched out wide, as if they could encircle the globe. When she went limp, he knew. Watched the squares below him broaden, like any other jump. Clutched the ripcord, timing the moment they would ease back down. Where the earth was waiting.

BOOK OF FACTS

As she hands him a beer and opens one for herself, she says, "Did you know, if you place a minute amount of liquor on a scorpion, it will instantly go mad and sting itself to death?"

He searches her eyes for clues. Does she know about him screwing around? Is that what this is about?

He shrugs.

"Well, it's true," she says. For several days now she's followed him about their small apartment, reading from a *Book of Facts*. And for weeks before that, he'd found her crazy doodles, in smeared red ink, everywhere. One, he recalled, looked like a man hanging by his testicles. But she'd insisted it was a dog on a leash, admittedly abstract, with big, bulging eyes. And another of a man's head, eerily familiar, circled by a swarm of angry eyes, scribbled on the edge of a shopping list. She told him, and with a straight face, they were *fireflies*. They were all just doodles. What'd he expect? They weren't going to wind up in the Louvre.

And now it was this: *Book of Facts*.

"Hey, here's one." She sits down at the kitchen table. Leaning against the fridge, he pulls his beer up, nearly empties it. She is still in her robe. He wonders what she does with her time, besides her artwork and torturing him with this cat-and-mouse. If she knows something, she should spill it.

"Lobsters," she reads. "*Do* feel pain when boiled alive. By soaking them in saltwater before cooking, however, you can anesthetize them."

"If it were only that easy," he says.

"Huh?" She looks up, takes a sip.

"The salt," he says. He's feeling antsy. He finishes his beer and tosses the can in the trash. Wonders what Laura is up to—needs to get out and clear his head. "There's some stuff I've got to do," he says. He goes into their bedroom and grabs his jacket.

"Did you know Louis XIV owned 413 beds?" she calls out. "Now why would anyone need so many? You'd think one would be enough."

Christ! He shakes his head. "I know what you mean," he calls back. "Kings—go figure. Look, I've got to leave for a bit." He glances in the dresser mirror, slips into his jacket, and combs his hair. "Some important documents I left at work. I've got a deadline." He heads back to the kitchen.

"What dead lions?" she says without looking up. She's bent over her outstretched arm on the table. He gazes at her pressing the red pen point against her forearm—sketching furiously, even grimacing once, as if she'd punctured the skin.

"*Deadline*," he repeats, from where he's suddenly stopped—trying to make out the image.

She finishes her drawing and looks up—smiles. "Only kidding," she says. "I heard you the first time." It's a smile, after all these years, he hasn't seen before. But it slides away quickly, like ice down a windshield. He stares at her drawing, thinking—*it can't be!* That *can't* be what it looks like.

She stands then, holding out her arm, eye level. "Sure," she says, and her old smile is back. "But before you go, come over here and look at my new tattoo."

FIRE AND ICE

He remembered looking through the windshield at a cloudless bright sky, befuddled by the suddenly buckling-in roof of his old VW Bug. The baseball-sized hailstones he imagined, battering down. When he turned, he saw his wife in her fuzzy robe—the golf club over her head—his. The cell phone dropped from his hand. A tinny voice on speaker saying, "Peter. . . *Peter*. . ." It was weather he knew was coming. Ice, after all, he'd shaped himself. He hoped she wouldn't get to the windows before he had a chance to start the car. The crushing irony of it all. The sun: making him squint. The ice: making him shudder.

SOMETHING FOR HENRIETTA

The woman slipped from the bed, then cried out as she stepped on the infant's head, "Damn! Damn! Damn!"

The little girl hurried in and pointed. "She said a bad word, Daddy. And stepped on Henrietta."

The woman hopped back to the bed and sat, rubbing the indentation in the sole of her foot. The father rose from the covers and wiped a bit of goop from one eye. "Now, what?" he said.

The little girl crouched down on the rug. She took the tiny plastic baby she'd gotten from a Cracker Jacks box and put it back inside the halved toilet paper tube, which served as a cradle, and rocked it. The woman glared down at her, at the fifty or so different improvised items that were gradually eating up the floor space in the father's bedroom.

"My foot," the woman said. "I stepped on that goddamn thing again."

"She said another bad word," the girl accused.

"You okay?"

The woman began dressing.

"Ooh, I see your butt," the girl said.

"I've had it," the woman said.

The man patted her side of the bed. "Come on."

The girl stretched out on the rug and repositioned an aluminum foil swing set, a pizza disc table, and the empty cigarette box that was Henrietta's dog crate. The actual dog was made of clay—twice mashed underfoot, and reconfigured. There was always something the girl seemed to be adding to Henrietta's world.

"Look, I need a little time," the woman said. After she put on her high heels, she opened a pack and lit a cigarette.

"Not in the house," the man said.

"Screw that," said the woman, and before the girl could speak, she said, "I know, another *bad word* from the *bad lady.*"

"Don't talk like that." The man patted the bed again. But the woman just stood there and tapped ash into her palm. The night before, she had tried to win over the girl by making chocolate chip cookies (from a family recipe). But when the girl took a bite, and made a twisted face like she was being poisoned, the woman threw up her hands. When the girl picked out the chips and said they could be Henrietta's poop, and tore off a piece of paper towel for a diaper, the woman tramped out of the kitchen.

"Can we have a minute?" the man told his daughter.

"I don't need a minute," the woman said. When she passed by the little girl, she pulled the thin cellophane band from her cigarette pack, and let it drift down. "Here," she said, "a jump rope for Henrietta."

"I'll call you," the man said in her wake. Then the door slammed.

"She already has a jump rope," the girl said.

"I know sweetie," the father said. He got up from the bed and looked out the window. He watched the woman drive off. He opened the window and sat on the edge of the bed facing it, and lit a cigarette.

"What are we doing today, Daddy?"

"Don't know, honey. I was thinking maybe the playground, the merry-go-round."

"Yippee," the girl said, hugging him around the neck. He blew smoke out of the corner of his mouth, away from her. The girl detached and glanced down. "Look," she said, reaching into a small trash can by the bed. She pulled out a torn-open condom foil. "A sleeping bag for Henrietta."

"No," the father said, coughing out some smoke, and taking it from her. Then, "*No, no*, not that either."

CRAZY HATS

She made crazy hats (his word for them) that were works of art. That two galleries on either coast were selling. Flamingo-crested bonnets, skyscraper fedoras. . . Brilliantly colored and sculpted sky-high.

A fly came in through the window and landed on their son's atlas, open on the rug. He turned from her latest creation she modeled with a sassy hip-raise. Watched the fly traverse a continent, an ocean. Then zip off to buzz fecklessly against the pane. "Well?" she said, under a fish tank sun hat of exotic platys swirling in still life. "Great," he told her. "Very cool." There was auto dirt rimming his fingernails he could never remove completely, and stopped trying. Beefy hands. One wrapped around a beer bottle.

The fly crawled inches from the open space, then battered against the corners of the frame. When he was young he wanted to study medicine. Thought he did. But schoolwork hurt his brain most times, so he took a trade. Never forgot that dead cat he found in an empty lot when he was twelve. How he wondered at the machinery inside it. Took a broken piece of glass and scored it along its matted fur, again and again, to solve the mystery. When a woman stuck her head out a window and called him a *fucking freak!* he dropped the glass and ran.

His wife grabbed another hat to show him. A skier-down-a-snowy-mountain cowboy hat. The fly crept to the edge of freedom, found the opening and flew out. He was relieved he didn't have to smash it.

The fog was coming in from the ocean and he got up to close the window. The little yapper one yard over was fading fast. Soon it would disappear altogether. Leaving only its bark and a few of the brightest roses.

FLY SWATTER

You find out an old friend was having a picnic by the shore, lifting a glass of Cotes du Rhone, when an out-of-control motorboat rockets from the lake and lands right the fuck on him.

You are ordering a talking Bible online (a Bible on tape) for your legally blind mother when the phone rings with the news, and the cat is rubbing your leg for those stinky stars that smell like fish, and sunlight is landing on the toaster— one heat turned on, the other off.

The shower's going and your wife is singing opera. Fucking opera. The clock is doing its thing over the fridge, a clock that never skips a beat, the fridge working behind closed doors. Consistent and unassuming. While the hand of God, or whatever, lifts a boat from the water like a soggy fly swatter and takes out a glass of wine and your best friend from high school. Who once told you he saw a Picasso bull while on LSD. Real as shit, but he went with it. Rode it out. Was a demolition expert in Iraq. Still with ten fingers and toes when he got out. Took over his father's pet shop. Really wanted to be a poet. But metaphors, he said, didn't pay the bills.

The talking Bible tells all the old stories your mother grew up on. You order it. Fill the cat's bowl. Your wife, with a towel twirled on her head, slips off stage into the bedroom. You put a couple of slices you'll never eat into the toaster. Needing normalcy. They pop up, predictably, transformed.

TRANSPLANT

It was so windy, it seemed to be blowing the crows from the trees. They'd caw their way with black swipes to a new perch, and then it would begin again. She sat in the lawn chair with her dress whipping against the aluminum frame, listening to her new heart, or trying to. What was Heavy Metal/John Cage was Mozart now. Her recovery had been slow but even. The scar, stunningly elegant. A long lifeline one might read in a palm and say, *Wow!* Some leaves skittered along the grass, then stopped against the fence like friction cars spun out. Her housedress shot way up, and she hoped that overeager neighbor of hers was looking. Two crows blew from a poplar, black smears from one yard to another. More leaves raced past her feet, as if they had somewhere to go.

LEANING IN

They stripped for each other on Skype, and he did a
simulated drum cymbals accompaniment with his tongue
against his teeth, a bit of spittle shooting out, as she tossed
her bra. The years hadn't been particularly kind. But they
oohed and *aahed* nonetheless.

Later, with their clothes back on, leaning in so close to
the screen their faces coned, they talked about their grown
children. How, with his young daughter on his shoulders
once at the circus, the man on stilts reached down to shake
her hand. How she squealed through the magic. How he
wished he had that photo. She told of her ex-husband's
obsession with huge cars. Especially Cadillacs. Their kids
as props beside them. How he kept stepping back and back
with his Polaroid, trying to fit them in, till the kids were
nearly smudges—door handle-sized against them. Albums
full. "Wow," he said.

When the talk waned, they stretched out the cords of
their Skype cameras and showed each other the natural light
that pushed in through their respective windows. Thousands
of miles apart. His light was a bit sunnier than her own. Her
window, blocked somewhat by a fat cat and a stained glass

fish dangling from the frame. There were streaks on his pane where rain had run down through the dust she'd never see. "Here, kitty-kitty," he said, pointing past her. Leaning in even closer, misunderstanding, she said, "*Meow*."

SCREAM

All day he fondled feet. Trapped them in high-end leather. Squeezed for toe tips and measured. Met several women that way. Was a B-movie monster many years earlier. Met his ex-wife on set. Had coffee with his monster head on the table and her shrill, one-take movie screams still in his head as they sipped and talked.

They had a son together who wanted a hermit crab for a pet when he was ten. Insisted on it. "A hermit crab," he told the attractive woman stretching out a leg and turning a red pump this way and that. "I had a turtle named Foxy," she said absently. He squeezed her toes and knew that was all he'd be squeezing.

"Plenty of room," he said. She got up and walked around to get the feel of them.

When he had sex with his wife (the screamer) she never made a sound. After five months of silence their hermit crab devotee was conceived. He bred miniature horses now on a ranch five states over. Sent postcards from time to time. The horses pictured on the front of them in fancy hand-tooled saddles. But the ink was usually smeared and they were hard to read.

"Foxy," he said, and she turned, smiled weakly. He wondered if she was a screamer. There were always too many contradictions to ever predict. If he'd learned anything, he'd learned that.

"I'll take them," she said. And he placed them back slowly in the box (north and south). In that whisper of tissue paper. Put a lid on it.

NOT EVEN ED SULLIVAN
COULD SAVE SUNDAYS

It was a lawn party in an upscale neighborhood filled with kids in pointy hats and their parents sipping drinks. I was part of a clown band. We played silly tunes, brassy and loud. I made my trombone sound like a giant farting. A single freckled boy laughed. And that was enough.

It seemed so much had slipped away. Not suddenly, like an avalanche. But one snowflake at a time melting against the pane. I made that sound again, but the freckled kid ran off without noticing. I gazed down at my watch. Had a date later in the evening. A gal from ChristianMingle.com—*Find God's Match for You!* I wasn't at all religious, but thought what the hell. I'd hedge my bets. Maybe a divine matchmaker was the ticket.

One of the drunken moms winked at me. I did some fancy riffs on my slush pump, then realized the wink was for Harold, the drummer behind me. Harold started beating the piss out of the snare, and she seemed to enjoy that. She spilled wine down the front of her dress and dabbed at it with a party napkin, slowing when she ran it over her breasts. Harold pounded the base drum like a heartbeat.

My father was a lush, and I remembered him on Sundays, staring down the barrel of another work week—whiskey running down his shirt. Saying once (between a yodeler and a spinning plates act) as we watched The Ed Sullivan Variety Show on TV, "Not even Sullivan can save Sundays."

The freckled kid came back with a girl in a polka-dot dress in tow. I giant-farted my trombone and they both looked up (at me this time) and giggled. It was enough.

A CONVERSATION WITH
THE FATHER I NEVER HAD

Life is a strop," my father says. "It sharpens us, especially in hard times."

"Isn't that a bit old-fashioned for a metaphor these days?" I say.

"Metaphors are timeless," he tells me. We are in a subway car hurtling through darkness. This man beside me, who once built a castle for our three-legged rescue dog, Stumpy, with crenulated walls, elegant and spacious in our small tenement apartment. So one of us could know what it felt like to be regal. I'm scraping up the Jackson Pollock puzzle pieces of myself after a ruinous divorce. He always liked puzzles, my father. Glued completed ones together and framed them. Put them up above the sofa, his overstuffed chair in front of the TV. Bucolic landscapes the roaches roamed.

"You can't serenade a woman in a snowstorm," he says, patting my shoulder.

"What the hell?"

"Wait for the weather to clear, is all I'm sayin'. There's someone out there worth the music."

He takes a cigarette out, but doesn't light it. He's carried the same full pack in his shirt pocket since he quit a decade ago. Puts the cigarette to his lips backwards, the filter pointing at my forehead. He was always a big man. Out the train window someone has painted against the wall (in bright white paint) a measured series of stick figures, which move in choppy motion like a flip book. Framed in the window glass as we zip by. They seem to be doing jumping jacks, or perhaps they are making love. They vanish too quickly for me to tell—an evaporating art.

My father takes the cigarette and pinches it between the fingers of one hand and then the other. Graceful as a magician. "Change does not come in a delivery truck with a strongman rolling it out at your doorstep," he says.

"And lightning has no cruise control when it strikes," I tell him.

He pauses, then puts the cigarette back in his mouth. The right way this time. It flaps up and down as he speaks. "You got that right," he says.

DEAR GOD (A LOVE STORY)

She's learned to yodel, and somehow listening to those rapid, fluctuating changes in pitch is turning me on. She's sitting by the window and her yodeling competes with a tree full of noisy birds, and a jet overhead, a garage band not nearly far enough away. She was once my wife and now she is just my daughter's mother. Everything in between has burned up in some desert when I wasn't paying attention, sucked up by some saguaro cactus, dangerously unapproachable.

She's good. The yodeling is good. And I can tell she's proud to be showing me this new useless prowess. And I wonder if it has the same effect on whoever the hell she's seeing at the moment. Those cherry red lips smiling now, and only the tree full of birds, the drum set and one screechy electric guitar remain.

"That's great," I say, thinking too bad there aren't any old Roy Rogers movies she could try out for. I'd love to get her back with some magnetic brilliance machine I haven't yet invented. See again what was once in those same eyes, only younger, that looked at me so differently. Want to tell her I feel like I just got a personal note from God that says, *You're screwed, pal!* when she asks how I'm doing.

"Great," I say. And there's those cherry red lips half-mooning up. I can hear our daughter singing in the next room as she gets her stuff. The weekends never last long enough and I will have to rememorize all the names she's given her extensive menagerie of stuffed animals. "Can you yodel a few lines from Shakespeare?" I ask.

"Always the kidder," she says and lifts her cup of coffee, which must be cold now. Then her cell lights up and blares a *Mission Impossible* ringtone. The garage band stops for what I'm sure must be a pot break.

"Excuse me," she says, and goes into the kitchen with the phone to her ear, laughing.

I write the Big Guy back in my head (simple and direct): *Dear God, WTF?!*

NUTS

The whole ride back from the flea market, he had that stupid look: the one where he was bursting like an overripe fig to tell her something, but wanted her to guess first.

"A bowling ball," she said, turning up the car radio to a favorite song by the Eagles. He lowered it as quickly.

"Nope," he said out of the corner of his mouth. "Use your imagination."

"Okay. A groupie's collection of plaster casts of famous rock stars' penises."

"Very funny," he said. "But actually you're not that far off. Geographically."

"You mean San Francisco, geographically? The rock scene there in the late sixties?"

"Cold," he said.

Christ, she thought. Now they were playing *Hot/Cold*. What, was he seven? She was beginning to get a headache. In the seat behind them were the three ferns she had purchased. No guesswork involved, and the bowling bag—his mystery bag—beside them.

"Come on Matt, just tell me."

"Don't be a quitter," he said.

And at that moment she wished *he* were a fern. She could talk to it as she clipped off its dead leaves. Maybe even sing to it, an Eagles song. Water it whenever she chose. Find the right spot for it, with just the right amount of light. Go about her life.

"Why do you use words like that?"

"Okay," he said. "Bulls' balls."

"What?"

"You heard me. Bulls' balls."

"Are you shitting me?"

"No, ma'am. I got a great deal on 'em."

She pictured a bloody bunch of testicles piled together in that bag, zipped tight. She didn't want to think about what he might have paid.

"Are you nuts?"

"Crazy like a fox," he said. He looked in the rearview. She followed his gaze, and turned. Glared at the bowling bag of dark perversion beside that leafy splendor.

"What the hell?" she said.

"They're dried," he told her. "Powdered. What'd you think they were, *farm fresh*?"

She rolled her window down. Needed some air. The Eagles were softly welcoming her to the Hotel California.

"I'm going to sell them in Chinatown. One of those exotic herb shops. They eat that shit up. Supposed to be an aphro-drisiac."

"Aphrodisiac," she corrected.

"Same difference."

She turned the radio up, but it was too late. The Eagles had put out their *No Vacancy* sign, and the song ended. But Matt had his neon *Another Harebrained Scheme* sign flashing in that smile of his. Blinking away in the dark.

PICTURING A RUTABAGA

Legally blind, she just listens to the TV now. It's like the radio, she says when I call. Ninety-one, and she still cooks for herself (don't ask me how), keeps the cleaning lady in line. Follows behind with an Inspector General's finger for dust. Tells me the city gave her a talking watch, but the thing went *batty*. Started talking to her at all hours.

Says she *pictures* things now. Looks out the window through the blur and sees winter branches in bloom. The framed faces on her dresser, the way she remembered them. Then out of the blue she says, "Rutabaga." Says she tried to think what a rutabaga looked like. I can hear the TV blasting in the background. I try to picture a rutabaga. Strain to recall if one ever made it into that shopping cart I pushed as a kid, with arms stretched up. The one she kept from banging into things. "They're round, I think," I tell her. Aware my eyes are shut. In our silence, I picture her picturing. For a long time only the TV is on the line between us.

WHAT ARE THE CHANCES?

Let's say, the skateboarders were back again, scraping up and down the empty swimming pool next door. There was the sharp, skunky scent of pot in the air, and we were on the deck watching the lemons on the tree yellow.

Let's say, we just got back home and the jewelry was missing, the window jimmied, and that large kitchen knife we kept in the drawer was on the bed. Our bed. That whoever took our stuff didn't need to use it. But held it just in case. It was still there. A shark in the waves of an unmade bed.

Let's say, I was more than a little annoyed that Camille was taking so frigging long picking through the aisles at Safeway on a sunny Saturday. Filling the cart, when I wanted it shallow. And what the hell was this thing about timing and luck anyway? A butcher knife in the hand/in the sheets/in the belly? The neighborhood kids on the other side of the hedges, oblivious—scraping, scraping. . .

Let's say, cancer never came at Kay Ballenger like a boulder down a mountain. And Joe didn't lose his job—everything—

and he was out there, instead of these rowdies, blackening barbecued ribs like he always did on weekends. And his wife, Kay, was by the pool in that blue sundress or on an inflatable in the water with a drink, her straw with lipstick at the end of it, her/our favorite shade of red. How it might have been different with their dog, Bruno, barking.

Let's say, that mockingbird was back in the poplars making a fuss with a throat full of stolen music, but I hardly heard it as we stared off, saying we needed to call the police. Needed to talk. One of the rowdies just said, "Fuckin' A!" after some kind of tricky maneuver, banging the hard wheels against the Spanish tiles Kay left wet butt prints against, I never forgot, just before she got up to dive back in. When the pool, so much, hadn't yet been emptied.

HIT MAN IN RETIREMENT

He awoke and dragged their bodies out of bed. He told himself it was the arthritis. Over coffee the voices were there (the usual suspects) some turning, startled, before a word could be uttered: the spray. Others begging—the big money offers, eyes bugged and jittery. One even offering his wife for a pass and a chance to leave the country.

But a job was a job, and what was a man if he couldn't do what he set out to do: be counted on. He glanced at the newspaper, some headlines, and shook his head with a *what's-the-world-coming-to* lopsided twist to his mouth. He looked forward to checking out the Obits.

There were some pigeons outside on the sill. They sounded like they were in love. He put out a few crumbs, but they fluttered off. They'd soon circle back. When he was younger he would have snapped their necks. He wondered if Janis would call. Thirty-two years apart and he still liked a word or two. All those years she never asked questions.

He slow-walked back to the kitchen—dragged a few bodies with him—their shoes scrapping along the linoleum.

A LEAFY HEFT

They were going through their mother's stuff. What was left of it. She decided she'd keep the monogrammed hankies. Remembered how her mother used them to dab a single tear sometimes. So artfully. They were ironed, neatly folded.

"Dainty," her brother said, opening empty drawers. Bending to look for money, anything of value that may have been taped under them. "Funny," he said, "how you never think about the snot seeing them like that."

She gave him a look.

There were posters of topiary art under their mother's bed, an elephant rising from the earth with leafy heft. A crocodile hedge, a swan. She opened them, gazed for a long time, then let them coil back, like muscle memory, into darkness. There was a box of unopened letters in the closet with old stamps on them. The brother reached out, but she slapped his hand away. He resumed dumping shoes in a plastic lawn bag, the pointy heels of some of them poking through. She buried her face in one of her mother's fancy church hats.

"You're weird," he said, ran his hand under a lifted mattress.

She wandered off.

There was a cracked plastic radio her mother listened to on the kitchen table, the unplugged cord dangling nearly to the linoleum. An ashtray from the Grand Canyon beside it. All those cheesy talk shows she and her mother tuned to. Her mother calling in on that pink Princess phone. That one program in particular, as they tapped away, filling the Grand Canyon with ash like a volcano. The host, some sort of talky shrink, she recalled, always responded, low and syrupy, saying: "I'm listening. . ."

SOMEWHERE BENEATH IT

There is a chipped-plaster Virgin Mary in the grotto out back. Panties on a line, small ones, big ones, and a large plaid shirt.

In the house something shatters. There are loud voices. A crow's shadow paints a handlebar moustache sliding down a drying white sheet as it passes. On the grass, a young girl is talking into a conch shell after putting an ocean to her ear. Somewhere beneath it is a mermaid who listens.

IT WILL LIFT YOU

The apartment is still filled with her cactuses. The potted prickers are everywhere. I could never get myself to rid the place of them. When we were together, she kept bringing home new ones. Before she left me and the dog to join a Christian rock band that toured the globe for Jesus. She can't sing a lick but can shake it pretty good and her guitar playing ain't half bad. Our (now my) dog, Stuart, is trying to fit two tennis balls in his mouth. The second pushing out the first each time. But he keeps trying. We are not so different.

She looks down. "You dumb cluck," she tells him. She has pink streaks in her hair and a large cross on a chain down the front of her. Rockin' for the Lord is big and she's in town pluckin' strings for the Big Fella. Wanted to "hook up." She scans the room, her eyes landing on each prickly sprouter in turn. I'm surprised she never gave them names. "You watering them?" she asks. "Not that they need much." The barrel cactus is in bloom. A look-but-don't-touch attraction. "I would have thought you dumped them by now." And I don't know why I haven't. It's like wading in a pool of piranhas most times.

"Perhaps I like the danger," I tell her and she smiles, fingering the gaudy cross.

"You going to catch our show?"

"Don't think so."

"You sure? The energy will lift you right up off the ground."

"I like the ground," I say. "I'm a big fan of the ground." I glance at her breasts, which are new. Pushing out that cross as it rests on one of them. Big boobs for Jesus, I think.

Stuart nearly has both balls in, but they shoot out together and he snaps after them. She heads into the kitchen and fills a glass with water and goes over to one of her plants. "Betsy is thirsty," she says, bending down. Her short skirt hitches up. Betsy, for Chrissake. And I never knew. Looking at her like that, I begin to feel frisky.

"You name those two in the bedroom?" I ask. She straightens, turns. I'm hoping that's not a godly look she's giving, but what I think it is.

"I'm happy you kept them," she says as we pass by, their needle teeth showing, and she grabs my hand. Past the dog still at it. Still trying to fit them in, the unfitable.

WISE SUNGLASSES

For years they kept the back door open so the dog could have access to the yard. There were spiders everywhere in the house because of it. Jumpers, small black ones, ones with red-tinted backs, which frightened her the most. It was just her and the dog now, pinballing through the rooms. And what remained of the spiders.

She had a lazy eye, which turned in a bit. Her sunglasses collection was vast. The heart-shaped pair were Pete's favorite. "My Lolita," he'd say, though she was far from it, and he'd find the real thing soon enough. But it made her feel young and maybe even a little coquettish for a time.

Later in the day she'd Skype with her daughter, a country away, wear the large round ones with silver owls attached to the temple stems. She'd thought of getting an owl tattoo twenty years earlier, when she was feeling sure and wise.

She shook out everything now: her clothes, towels. . . Carefully opened umbrellas to see what might swing out on a thread. Waited for Bosco to give her the "sad eyes" before letting him out. The back door shut tight. Kept a can of bug spray on all three counters. Saw a movie once (she couldn't shake it) where giant spiders took over a town. Came in from the desert. Because of nuclear testing they were mutated, big as Volkswagens ravaging the populace. Hairy with elephant tusk-sized pincers, opening and closing.

One time, Pete, on a lark, surprised her by coming into the bedroom wearing a glow-in-the-dark condom. It was neon green, and she laughed. When she turned on the light later, she saw one. With a reddish tinge, navigating the waves of their sheets. She screamed. They both began beating after it with her furry slippers. The first things handy. How creepy the bed felt after that.

She looked at herself, distorted, in the shiny steel side of her toaster, waiting for a slice to snap up. When she turned, Bosco was giving her "the look." She slipped on her owl sunglasses, not feeling the least bit wise, and slid open the back door.

PLINK!

It's hailing like crazy. Diamonds spilling down from the heavens. As a kid I collected them on my tongue (their small icy shocks).

Now, it's a racket. A pretty one. I look out the window, say, "What a view."

My wife hears, "*Wanna screw?*" and glances up from the stack of papers she's grading, her red pen suspended over critical scribbles—blood on the tracks.

"Are you serious? Can't you see what I'm doing here? How sexy is that?" She shakes her head and proceeds to deliver, even more emphatically, swift red slashes.

The dog farts and she reaches for the box of wooden matches on the coffee table, lights one without taking her eyes off the paper. Listens to the flame crackle for a moment, then snuffs it out with a snap of the wrist, directing the smoke at Uncle Wiggly.

I open the window and the diamonds are bounding everywhere—against the asphalt, the pebbled walks, off the slick backs of cars, a few even bouncing inside and blending into the syntax of my open book. Then it suddenly stops. The way magic often does.

Uncle Wiggly gets up, stretching his hind legs as he does, strides off to the toilet bowl for a drink.

WORTH TASTING

His aunt, Jen, had been a professional screamer. She'd grab her head, bug-eyed, and scream to the high heavens in low-budget horror movies of the fifties. In basements, dark woods, houses with floors that creaked. . .

Not long before her passing, she told him that butterflies *taste with their feet*. They were in her garden, a barren yard really, with a few shrubs and a bunch of beer cans she'd flung from the deck at the base of a tree. Giving the appearance it was a booze tree that had surrendered its fruit. She smoked stinky French cigarettes, her face severely wrinkled from old age and the many contortions it had endured. But it was amazingly calm—a life lived. At ease with an unfractured truth. Even as she coughed into the crook of her arm. Even as the cans emptied. Even as the butterflies flew past, nothing in her yard worth tasting.

ROBOTS IN THE WILD

"*La terra del rimpianto,*" I tell my sister, who says she is done with men. Done with all the drama and disappointments. She gulps down a Diet Pepsi. Is surrounded by sugarless food substances. Is at war with time's discourteous ways. There are more mirrors in her house than at the Palace of Versailles.

"What's that?" she says.

"The land of regret," I tell her. "You roam it freely."

"No shit," she says. "Don't we all?"

She opens the fridge and sticks her head inside. I'm wondering if she's got a mirror in there as well. Her most recent "dud" was a pharmacist who quit his job at Walgreens to do photography full-time, who, by her account, was obsessed with photographing the wild parrots of San Francisco drunk on juniper berries. And I picture them falling out of trees.

She pulls out another Diet Pepsi, drinks it as though she is putting out a fire. "I can pick 'em," she says.

"Maybe you could order one of those robots like they have in Japan. Something reliable. That doesn't come with an overactive camera, a drug problem, a wife, and is not a member of a biker gang. . ."

"Don't rub it in," she says and sits down at the kitchen table across from me.

"Maybe what I need is to nab one in the wild," she says.

"A biker?"

"A robot. Some uncomplicated guy out there that just wants to make me happy. Makes it his life's ambition."

I laugh, remember when we were kids and lived on the fifth floor of a tenement building. How all the building backs faced each other, crisscrossed by clotheslines. Attached to every window by a pulley. The excitement we felt as our mother reeled in our clothes in winter: our garments in frozen slabs. My pants like half of a steamrolled body. Her dresses like bells. How much simpler a time it was. How undeveloped our requirements were back then.

"Robots in the wild," I say. "I bet they're out there."

She ponders it for a moment, then jumps up, says, "*Borring*. I couldn't last two minutes with a stiff like that." She races to a mirror, fixes her hair. "I'm going to be late," she says. "Got a meeting. Could you let Edgar out? I don't want him peeing on the rug again."

"Sure," I say, but think how good it would have been to tell her all about me and Sandra. How shaky things have been. Maybe joke about how I could bag a robot in the wild myself. How I might like that. One that didn't slink around behind my back. How all the pieces might fall in place. But all I am these days for her is a full-length mirror, and reflection, not self-reflection, is what she's after. "We'll talk later," I say.

"You bet," she says, and leaves.

I stare for a long time at a framed photo (which is really quite good) of some wild berry-drunk parrots fluffing out a tree before I slide the back door open and let Edgar out into all that light.

MEDICAL RECORDS

It was a job I had in my twenties, buried deep, where you could see fat robins hopping about through the windows high overhead. All that joy, all this paper pain below. A bank of filing bins on rollers filled with charts. The thousands of knife blades that struck/the close calls. . . Lab reports and scribbled Latin in every shade of black and blue. Charts we'd read sometimes like supermarket tabloids. Shared. Dumbwaiters ferrying them back and forth. Quick hands at either end.

On the wall a poster of a nun high in the air above a trampoline, her habit billowing up her thighs, that Phil taped there. Our jester at the foot of the gallows. This place.

His recording studio we'd go to after work. Where we'd drink ourselves blind. A basement room with egg crate walls. Two guitars against them and a standing mic raised higher than either of us. Big dreams and silence hissing out.

One time, Phil playing air guitar between the giant bins. Between Simmons and Tremont. Between life and death. That tight space where you hit all the right notes. Where there were no strings to break.

THE ROOM NEXT DOOR

There was a porno movie being filmed in the motel room next door. They were sure of it. Earlier they'd seen the cameraman walk in, a man hauling floodlights, and then two men, and what looked like a hooker wearing a cheap, Cleopatra-style blonde wig.

They were making the long drive to visit his parents. There was sunshine waiting and a big swimming pool. And there'd be decades-old tunes piped out (poolside) to hum to.

The motel walls were thin and when the grunts and *oh, yes*es began to well up from the common wall, she hovered over the phone between the two beds. "I think we should call the desk and complain," she said, with that sour face she broke out from time to time, reminiscent of those nights (strung together) when he'd come home late from work and she'd slap a TV dinner on the table and tell him he knew where the microwave was.

"Disgusting," he said. "But I don't know if we want to cause a ruckus."

"A ruckus?"

"You know, maybe the police getting involved. Something like that."

"*Yeah, like that. . .*" The woman's syrupy voice oozed through the wall. And he thought: skin and sweat. Close-ups. . .

"You mean it's illegal?" she said.

"I don't know. Could be."

She was in that blue dress he liked and they were about to head out for dinner. "Why don't you wear that pearl necklace you got at the flea market," he said.

"You know they're not real."

"Who cares," he said. "They don't have pearl police out here." She liked that.

A man from the other side of the wall said something they couldn't make out, and the woman in the blonde wig said something back with the syrup left out this time. Then there was a lot of panting, and some dirty talk they *could* make out.

"I always liked that dress," he said. "And the pearls." He looked at her for a moment. "The pearls, even without the dress."

She turned toward the wall. There was the steady rapping of a headboard against it.

"You hungry?" she said. "You were so keen on Mexican earlier."

"Not so much."

There was a Bible on the end table. She put it in the drawer and eased it shut.

"Maybe we should put on the TV," she said. "To drown them out."

"Maybe," he said. He had one foot in and one out of his trousers.

"This is disgusting," she said, after she rustled a hand down deep into her suitcase.

"I know," he said, and she was standing there with just the pearls on. The fake pearls, in the dim light. Just enough to make them real.

HOW TO BUILD A GOD

A friend comes over with a book on how to build a god. He has read many such books he clings to. Books with heft and wings, which never leave the ground. My wife is by the window playing an intricate piece on harp, the lovely notes in contrast to the crows outside with their harsh, monosyllabic utterings. She waves when he comes in: a midway grace between an uninterrupted pluck.

"Nice," he says, and she smiles. The crows, with their harsh esthetic seem less impressed. He was a riveter at the Oakland Naval Yards years earlier and I wonder if that skill will come in handy with such god building. But metaphors are wimpy when it comes to such hardy applications. They are mist and vapors, when you need a hammer's grip.

He reads a passage, slowly, looks up at me. "I'm just sayin'," he says. He has all his ex-girlfriends' names tattooed down one arm, with a black tattoo line through each: a permanence highlighting impermanence.

I try to recall the name of the piece my wife is playing. Go through an alphabet in my head to retrieve it. Think it begins with a "D." Perhaps: "S." Hell, it could be any one of them. It suddenly means so much. Getting this or that right. *Knowing*.

But the crows, the crows seem to understand something we do not. That sticks. Branch to branch, perhaps. With a single screech against the silence. The only page they turn.

THE INTERVIEW

Sometimes Stan felt he was walking through a boxed canyon. With every likelihood of an ambush. His socks were gray, his suit blue, and his tie had red stripes angled like whiplashes. The interview was on the top floor. Everything was riding on it. A young man beside him with his hat on backwards moved a toothpick around in his mouth like a baton to the elevator Muzak. Stan wanted a hat like that to wear backwards. Someone old kept pressing the "Close" button at every stop, again and again and again and again. With no effect on the outcome whatsoever.

SAFE

For years, she told me, she was the human equivalent of a Swiss Army knife. Until she wasn't. Till all that was left was the blade. We were talking about exes. X-ed out exes. On a crunchy blanket at the beach. "Friends with benefits." Nothing more. Under the screeching gulls and our coconut-scented protective shells against the sizzle.

I told her how my mother sewed parachutes in a factory during the war. How my father parachuted into breakfast, into interrupted conversations. Into a stale momentum. Till the air went out, and the silk collapsed—burlap hanging from the high branches. How my own exes were less like startled birds and more like slow-moving lava down a mountain. There was time to pack a bag.

We slicked each other's backs and swiped at sandflies. Our friendship/our open borders as equitable a protection. But I couldn't help but wonder what *more* might look like, and wondered if she wondered. There were Frisbees, and dogs, and kids encircled in foam and seaweed. There were what-ifs beneath the gulls.

She rolled over and into a novel. I pulled my hat down, drew in the small, merciful coolness from its shade. Reminded myself to unwrap every meager gift. A gull stole something from a neighbor a few blankets down and flew off. There was a sea full of fish it landed at the edge of. It stood there and ate it.

MARTIANS,
CHILI LIME PISTACHIOS, AND
WHAT WAS LEFT OF MY FATHER

The Jehovah's Witnesses had hacked their way fruitlessly through the jungle with the sharp edges of their beliefs, trying to get to us. But we'd managed to send them packing. We were eating chili lime pistachios when they came to the door. A giant bagful. We decided we'd eat them till our tongues were numb. Tina looked up from the supermarket tabloid our daughter had left behind, said, "Jo-hos are a kind of mental abuse. They never quit." There were a couple of Martians on the tabloid cover that looked like they were doing Pilates.

"I know," I told her. "I think I have a Jesus migraine. The beginning of one at least. I wanted to throttle the one in the blue suit."

"They both had blue suits."

"Okay, both of them," I said. "I wanted to throttle both of them."

We decided we'd toss the shells onto the hardwood floor. Just for the hell of it. To be bad. We'd clean it up later, we told ourselves. It was liberating. I was going through a small box of my father's "personals" my stepmother sent me. He was gray bone-stones and flakes now. A giant man reduced in an urn you could shake like a rattle.

I pulled out a Nixon campaign tie and put it on. Added a few shells to the rubble. Tricky Dick smiled from my chest. Bruno came over and sniffed the floor as well as he could, scrapping his Elizabethan collar through the mess, then bumped off, disgusted, into furniture to get to his food bowl.

Tina looked over. "You okay?" she asked. I nodded that I was.

I pulled out an old watch from the box, a bunch of pens and pencils banded together, a tin can filled with old pennies, a magnifying glass. The one he used to do newspaper puzzles (denying he ever needed glasses). Some photos of him in uniform smiling with a rifle, smiling with a son, smiling in front of a long blue Cadillac. . .

"Maybe those Jo-hos were Martians," Tina said. "You read this crap, you begin to wonder." I grunted. She spilled out a handful of pistachios and pried them open with her fingernails, methodically. Flung the shells. All that effort for such a meager prize. I took the bag and tipped it into my hand/my father's hand with those wispy hairs just below the knuckles. Tina looked at me as though she wanted to say something, but didn't. There was still more in the box, but I put it down. Our tongues were still far from numb, but there was half a big bag left, and we were working on it.

A UNICORN, A CHICKEN, AND GOD SPEAKING THROUGH MY MOTHER'S CAT

We were on a carousel talking above the calliope music. She on a saddled chicken and I on a unicorn I remembered from my youth. She was chewing a wad of gum (three sticks' worth) with her mouth open, as she molar-mashed it vigorously, which I wasn't too crazy about.

When we got circling pretty fast, she leaned way over and made a lewd gesture with her hand, up and down the unicorn's horn, and grinned.

"Don't," I said, looking around to see if any children were watching.

"Think how magical *that* would be," she said.

"What would be?"

"Forget it," she said. She pulled back onto the chicken, pouting, and I couldn't tell whether it was a faux pout or the real thing.

Earlier that day my sister had called and said our mother thought God was talking to her through her old cat, Trixie. I wondered what God could possibly be telling her between licking its ass and strafing fleas. My sister and I were beginning to use the H-word. During more stable times, my mom had me promise I wouldn't dump her in a home. "Take me out behind the barn and shoot me first," she'd said. We didn't have a barn, but I got her drift. It was a promise I wanted to keep.

"I was just kidding around," she said, this thirty-seven-year-old-going-on-sixteen chicken jockey I'd met on *JustforFun.com*. Thought it might be. But it wasn't. I wasn't. The carousel was her idea. We haggled over the unicorn, and I'd won. What we did next, we decided, would swing in her favor.

"I know," I said, "but the kids. . ."

"They have no idea what any of it means. I could have been polishing the thing for all they know."

"You're right," I told her. "I need to lighten up." She liked that. Swept a few strands of hair from her face and grinned again. It had been a little more than a year since the divorce, and it still seemed, most times, like I had to stand on tiptoe just to keep my head above the waves.

She took her cell phone out and flashed a selfie. "Facebook," she said, and I could see that gum in there. She pointed the phone at me and I smiled, feeling phony doing it. Wondered what, if anything, she wanted to do next. What "fun" thing.

When Trixie was a kitten, she'd bat a grape around the kitchen floor, chasing it. My mom got such a kick out of that. Never imagined Trixie would someday be a hot mic for the Lord. I took out a pen and scribbled in my notebook: *pick up kibbles for cat.*

She snapped another selfie, giving the chicken finger-horns. "You writing me a poem?" she said. "You're a poet, right?"

I nodded. "An epic," I said, lowering a leg as the carousel slowed, and the bored older man pulled back a lever to bring it all to a halt.

A PURGATORY DWELLER'S
GUIDE TO BIRD-WATCHING

You come home from work with a tale to tell. For the kids. The wife. What happened on the elevator. . . How you. . . The phone rings. The oven timer rings. The TV drowns you out. And the only thing that saves the day, besides the six-pack patient in the fridge, is when you walk the dog and turn at just that right moment. See a sparrow, high above the tree line, dive as Edgar lifts a leg. Fifty-caliber-bullet fast, landing inside a diamond in a chain link fence a foot away. Framed there for a moment, with a single eye on you, in a twitchy, angled head. Then just as quickly, it jets off. Taking you with it.

Robert Scotellaro has published widely in national and international books, journals and anthologies, including W.W. Norton's *Flash Fiction International, NANO Fiction, Gargoyle, New Flash Fiction Review, Matter Press, The Laurel Review,* and many others. His stories were included in *Best Small Fictions* (2016 and 2017) and *Best Microfiction 2020.* He is the author of seven literary chapbooks, several books for children, and four full-length story collections: *Measuring the Distance, What We Know So Far* (winner of The 2015 Blue Light Book Award), *Bad Motel,* and *Nothing Is Ever One Thing.* He was the recipient of *Zone 3*'s Rainmaker Award in Poetry. He has edited, along with James Thomas, *New Micro: Exceptionally Short Fiction* published by W.W. Norton & Company (2018). He is one of the founding donors to The Ransom Flash Fiction Collection at the University of Texas, Austin. Robert lives with his wife in San Francisco. Find him online at www.robertscotellaro.com.

CPSIA information can be obtained
at www.ICGtesting.com
Printed in the USA
LVHW091259270920
667207LV00006B/1975